CRAZY GAMES

Sandra Glover

CORGI BOOKS

CRAZY GAMES

A CORGI BOOK 0552 548030

First published in Great Britain by Andersen Press Limited

Andersen Press edition published 2002
Corgi edition published 2003

1 3 5 7 9 10 8 6 4 2

Copyright, © 2002 by Sandra Glover

The right of Sandra Glover to be identified as the author of this
work has been asserted in accordance with the Copyright, Designs
and Patents Act 1988

Papers used by Random House Children's Books are natural,
recyclable products made from wood grown in sustainable forests.
The manufacturing processes conform to the environmental
regulations of the country of origin.

Set in 12/14½ pt Bembo by FiSH Books, London WC1

Corgi Books are published by Random House Children's Books,
61-63 Uxbridge Road, London W5 5SA,
a division of The Random House Group Ltd,
in Australia by Random House Australia (Pty) Ltd,
20 Alfred Street, Milsons Point, Sydney, NSW 2061, Australia,
in New Zealand by Random House New Zealand Ltd,
18 Poland Road, Glenfield, Auckland 10, New Zealand,
and in South Africa by Random House (Pty) Ltd,
Endulini, 5A Jubilee Road, Parktown 2193, South Africa

THE RANDOM HOUSE GROUP Limited Reg. No. 954009
www.kidsatrandomhouse.co.uk

A CIP catalogue record for this book is available from
the British Library.

Printed and bound in Great Britain by
Bookmarque Ltd., Croydon, Surrey.

CHAPTER ONE

Brad knew every centimetre of the Core. He knew where to run and he knew where to hide. But the cops were closing in.

Staying close to the blackened walls of the derelict buildings, Brad made his way through the rubble of what had once been a thriving city centre. Decay had crept slowly at first, as the banks, offices and shops began to close, no longer needed as more and more transactions were made on the Net.

The Core had become the haunt of the old, the poor, the techno-phobes, the undesirables, the revolutionaries. Until the government had decided to act, eliminating the growing dangers, bombing this city centre and a dozen others to the ground.

Brad's muscles tensed, his fingers tight on his gun, as two figures appeared, shuffling out of the blackness. Bent, wrinkled figures whose gaunt faces and wide, hungry eyes called out to him silently. Geriatrics.

It would have been a kindness to pull the trigger. Once. Twice. Two clean shots to the head and their suffering would be over. But he didn't. He hurried on. He couldn't afford to waste ammunition. The Geriatrics posed no threat. They just gave you a bit of a scare, sometimes. But they were usually harmless.

Despite the bombing there were still thousands of

people scattered amongst the ruins. Desperate people. Dangerous people, with axes, machetes, knives.

Brad had used his own knife to steal a gun. A knife was a good enough weapon, if your reflexes were fast and your victim stupid. But guns were better. Cleaner. Quicker.

You could kill cops with guns. Cops were the real enemy. The ones you had to watch. The ones who were hunting down the survivors of the original blast.

Survivors like Brad who'd spent all his time since the bombing searching the rubble for stuff to sell. Stealing. Fighting. Killing cops, when he got the chance.

The trouble was, for every dead cop they parachuted in another half dozen. And once you were known as a 'rogue', a cop killer, you became a named target yourself. Top of the list. Priority kill.

Five cops had been trailing him since early morning. He'd lost one and killed one. So three now. Out there. Not far away.

'If you get lost ask a policeman.'

Words from long ago. Words his granddad had said to him once when they'd been at a crowded football match.

'Keep hold of my hand, Brad. But if anything happens, if we get split up, if you get lost, ask a policeman.'

He couldn't have been more than six then. Funny that the words should suddenly come back to him, reminding him of real policemen in blue uniforms, who were kind to lost children. Not these guys with their hidden faces and heavy duty weapons. They were different. Impersonal killing machines . . . if you didn't get them first.

Brad slipped into a building which had once been a major department store. Nothing much remained but there was still part of a stairway, at the back. From there, you could pull yourself up and crawl across a section of blasted-out wall into something which more or less resembled a room. A hideout he'd used before.

From the high room, he looked down, searching for cops. Desperate to become again the hunter, not the hunted. To turn the game around. That's what gave you the kicks.

He yawned and blinked. So tired now, he could barely focus. Shadows, shapes, real and imagined, assaulted his eyes. Sounds came out of nowhere, bombarding his ears. The throbbing beat of music, far-off screams . . .

'Brad!'

His name being called. Distant. Detached. Repeated.

'Brad!'

Concentration momentarily blitzed. Eyes which had almost closed, jolted open.

Swinging round, Brad saw them. Two grey figures. He'd failed to watch his back, thought Brad, cursing himself. Big mistake. Fatal mistake.

Both cops fired in unison. Brad didn't stand a chance. His whole body throbbed in one last, dramatic movement. Dying was the biggest kick of them all.

Nick stared at his brother's limp body and pallid face. Carefully he lifted the 3D visor from Brad's eyes.

'Brad,' he said. 'Brad!'

The eyes blinked. Brad looked up to see Nick's face gazing down at him.

'Brad, are you OK? You look sort of strange.'

'That's because I've just been shot! Now bog off, Nick. I've told you not to come in here.'

'I knocked.'

'I don't care whether you announced your arrival by playing the National Anthem on the bagpipes, I don't want you in my room, OK?'

'What are you doing anyway?'

'Cutting my toe-nails.'

Nick looked around for signs of discarded socks and nail scissors, before he realized it was one of Brad's little jokes.

'Must be a good game,' he said, looking at the frozen screen. 'I said your name five times, before you heard me.'

'It was a good game before you came and ruined it, you little heap of—'

'"Survival",' said Nick, picking up the box. 'Where d'yer get that from, then?'

'It's none of your business,' said Brad, snatching the box and taking a swipe at Nick with it.

'Mum'll do her nut, if she sees it. It's an 18. I saw it on the box.'

'Clever boy, Nick,' said Brad. 'Recognizing numbers before your ninth birthday! You'll be learning to add up next.'

'You won't think it's funny when I tell Mum. And I'll tell her about that too,' he said, pointing at what Brad was wearing. 'I know what it is!'

'If you tell Mum anything,' said Brad, grabbing Nick's arm and twisting it up his back, 'I'll break your arm, right?'

'Geroff, Brad,' Nick whined. 'That hurts.'

'It's meant to,' said Brad, giving it a final tug before letting go. 'Anyway, what do you want?'

'Sunil's here. He said I could play footie with you, if I came up and got you. Save him taking his trainers off.'

'We're not playing footie,' said Brad. 'Specially not with you. Tell Sunil to come up. I want to show him something.'

'You're gonna show him the game,' said Nick, brightly. 'Can I watch?'

'No. I've told you. Bog off.'

The sound of Nick's footsteps tramping miserably downstairs was immediately followed by quicker, lighter ones.

'Hey, Brad,' said Sunil. 'Why don't you want to play footie? It's really nice out. Well, for the middle of November! And I promised your Nick...Flips! You didn't tell me you'd got a Blast-Pac.'

He strode over to the swivel chair where Brad was sitting and touched the padded shoulders of the black, sleeveless jacket, which Nick had noticed earlier.

'Careful,' said Brad, laughing. 'You'll kill me. They're dead sensitive.'

'What does it feel like?' said Sunil. 'Do they really jolt your body when you get shot? Are they as good as they make out?'

'Better,' said Brad. 'Absolutely unbelievable! Or too

believable. Thing is, you can't play the game properly 'cos half the time, you're sort of hoping to get killed just to feel the blast. It's incredible. Like your heart's exploding. I keep expecting it to spurt right out of my chest and splatter on the screen.'

'Cool,' said Sunil. 'But how the heck did you talk your parents into it? Did your dad win the lottery or something? Or is this a pressie for getting into all the top sets this year, you great swot?'

'I wish!' said Brad. 'I'll have to wait another hundred years or so till they come down in price a bit. This is Colford's. He got it for his birthday.'

'He didn't tell me!' said Sunil. 'I asked him what he'd got and he said a game. "Survival". I don't reckon he has, though. Not "Survival".'

'He has,' said Brad, flashing the box. 'He got the flamin' Pac and the game.'

'How?' said Sunil. 'They're not releasing it here, are they? It's supposed to be too gory. Too realistic.'

'It's realistic, all right,' said Brad. 'And in 3D it's incredible. But it's not what you'd call gory. Can't see what the fuss is about. It's bound to get in the shops sooner or later.'

'But not yet?' said Sunil. 'So how come Col's got it?'

'Need you ask?' said Brad. 'It's his dad. You know what he's like for getting his hands on stuff. I bet he got the Pac through those shady mates of his. He never pays full price for anything.'

'Maybe that's why Col didn't mention it,' said Sunil.

'If he knows it's stolen goods.'

'I didn't say it was stolen, exactly,' said Brad. 'And Col didn't mention it 'cos I told him not to. The minute he starts blabbing about it, everyone'll want to borrow it.'

'And you wanted to get in first?'

''Course,' said Brad, grinning.

'You were pretty quick off the mark, weren't you?' asked Sunil. 'His birthday was only two days ago. Thursday, wasn't it?'

Brad nodded.

'Bet he hasn't had a chance to use it himself yet, has he?'

'No, well, something this good'd be wasted on Col, wouldn't it?' said Brad, grinning again. 'He didn't have a clue how to set it up. So I said I'd get it going for him. Test it out. Make sure it worked. Want a go?'

'You bet!'

Brad took off the Blast-Pac jacket, showed Sunil how to put it on, made sure it was connected up properly, handed over the 3D visor and re-set the game. Let Sunil start from scratch. Right at the first level, finding his way through the decaying city, avoiding the beggars, druggies and other dross who lurked there. Learning the routes. Picking up goods, points and weapons which could be used later, at level two, when the city had been blasted and things started to get really mean.

He'd only got to level three himself. Getting rid of the cops covered several levels. After that, according to *Virtuality* magazine, you went on to meet the zombies. All the low life who'd been killed in the city blasting, revitalized by the putrid mix of chemicals seeping from the punctured sewers. It was a great game.

Nick had been right though. Best not to let Mum see it. Not after the fuss she'd made when Stacey's brother, Steve, brought 'Ulti-Max' round the other week. She'd glanced at the back of the box Steve had plonked on the coffee table and told him he could take it straight back home, thank you very much. And it was only rated 15! Mild, by anybody's standards, Brad mused. Anybody, that is, except his mum.

'It might be all right for you,' she'd told Steve. 'You're nearly eighteen. Brad's only fourteen. There's a big difference.'

Embarrassing or what? Especially with Stacey sitting there, grinning at him! He'd be fifteen on Boxing Day and the chances were that Mum still wouldn't let him buy the older games. Honestly, thought Brad. What did she expect? Did she think he wasn't smart enough to know the difference between games and reality? Did she really think he'd pop into town and massacre the three blokes who made up the local police force, just because he'd played 'Ulti-Max' or 'Survival'?

'Aaaaaaagh!'

'Don't do that!' said Brad as Sunil screamed and writhed on his chair. 'You scared me to death.'

'Well, you should have warned me,' said Sunil. 'I wasn't expecting it. I thought the Pac was only for gun-fire. You didn't say it worked when you got stabbed.'

'It does, but it's a different sensation. Sort of fainter and only in one spot.'

'Fainter?' said Sunil. 'I don't think I'll bother with the guns, then.'

'Give us a go,' said Brad. 'These are gonna get better and better, I reckon,' he said, as he took the Pac from Sunil. 'At the moment, you only get to feel the stab wound in one place. It's always to the middle of your back, belting right through to your chest. Eventually, they'll make 'em so's you can feel wounds in the shoulder, legs, everywhere. And they're working on a Blast-helmet that'll let you feel bullets right through the head.'

'I'm not sure I'd fancy that,' said Sunil.

'Wimp,' said Brad, getting a tight grip on the controls before entering his pass code.

When he returned to reality, Brad was aware of not one, but two people in the room. His recently blasted heart missed a beat, as the horrible thought that it might be his mother clicked in.

He swivelled round, pushing back his visor. Safe. It was only Dad. Dad didn't get too worked up about the games. He played them himself sometimes. He understood.

'I don't like the look of that, Brad.'

Usually.

'Why?' said Brad, wondering how long Dad had been standing there, watching. 'What's wrong with it? It's no worse than "Carnage".'

'I don't like the way it seems to target specific groups. Beggars. Old people. The police, for heaven's sake!'

Obviously been watching a while, then. You couldn't get the full impact of the game without the visor but his dad had obviously seen enough.

'Yeah, but they're not real cops,' said Brad. 'The country's become a police state. They've just blitzed all the old cities! These are the bad guys.'

'But the mere fact that the game identifies the police as the bad guys seems a bit iffy to me,' said his dad.

'I get what you mean, Mr Bradshaw,' said Sunil. 'It might change the way you react to real cops. Make you more aggressive towards them.'

'Whose side are you on, Sunil?' said Brad. 'Lighten up, you two. It's a GAME.'

Brad's dad didn't comment on the Blast-Pac. He probably thought it was the latest fashion item from Nike, thought Brad, not bothering to enlighten him. His dad didn't like him borrowing expensive stuff from people. Especially not Colford. Not since two years back when Brad had accidentally crashed Col's racing bike into a wall. Col's dad had come round and there'd been a heck of a stink. They'd had to pay for a new bike and Brad had been grounded for a month.

'I don't mind the games where you're killing monsters and aliens,' his father was saying to Sunil. 'Or the fantasies where it's all knights and wizards. But real people make me a bit uneasy.'

'So you won't be buying Brad a Game-Scan then?'

'No chance!' said Brad. 'Have you seen the price of them? We'd have to mortgage the farm.'

'We'll have to mortgage the farm, just to pay the bills,' muttered his father, bitterly. 'If things don't get better soon. So, no. I don't suppose I'll be buying you a . . . whatever it is.'

'Game-Scan,' Sunil repeated. 'You know! Where you can put pictures of real people into your games. So if Brad was being a pain, I could scan him into "Doom-View" and zap him!'

'Whatever next!' said Mr Bradshaw. 'Game-Scans, 3D visors, Inter-actives and those awful jackets they've just brought out.'

Brad shuffled, trying to rest his hands on his knees to hide the telltale wires of the jacket.

'And I remember the days when we thought "Lemmings" was pretty neat,' continued Brad's father, sighing wistfully.

Brad didn't remember 'Lemmings', but he remembered having a laugh at Dad's old 'GameBoy'. Tiny little screen. Fuzzy black and white images. Technology had certainly moved on fast. There was no way you could keep up with all the latest stuff, unless you were Colford. But it was always worth a try.

'If we had a Game-Scan,' said Brad, 'you could scan that cop, who did you for speeding, into "Carnage" and get your own back!'

'Sounds tempting,' said his father, laughing. 'Hang on. Is that the phone?'

A moment later Nick's voice yelled up the stairs.

'Brad. It's Colford. For you.'

'Idiot,' Brad hissed, as he pushed past his brother in the hall. 'Why didn't you say I was out?'

CHAPTER TWO

Brad left the house at 7.46 precisely on Monday morning. Sunil would leave at 7.44 and they would meet at the junction of the two dirt tracks, near Mr Brown's cottage. They would walk the half mile or so to the bus stop on the main road.

They would be the only two passengers waiting, the only two pupils at Barnaby Merrick High to come from Tringle Nook. What a name for a village! Brad had always been embarrassed by his name and address. Lawrence Bradshaw, Primrose Farm, Tringle Nook. Well, you could change your name. From the minute he'd learnt to speak, he'd insisted on Brad. But the address! It sounded like a retirement home for garden gnomes.

Until five years ago, Brad had been the only kid in the village, unless you counted his brother, Nick, which he didn't. Then three more had arrived at once when Sunil's family had moved into Harry Tappit's recently converted barn.

There were once two working farms in the village. Theirs and Harry's. But times had changed. Farmers had been struggling since before the turn of the century and Harry was getting on. He was seventy-four when he gave up. He converted two of his fields into a caravan park and sold the rest, using some of the money to turn his barn into a house.

House prices had been on the rise and rumour had it that he'd made a tidy profit. The newcomers caused quite a stir amongst the eleven households, of mainly elderly people, who made up the village, or technically the hamlet, of Tringle Nook.

'Have you seen them?' the whisper had gone round, in the weeks before Sunil's family moved in. 'They're Asians!'

If they'd been Pea-Green Space Spiders with red, hairy legs, they could hardly have caused more gossip. But it wasn't so much prejudice, Brad now realized, as total ignorance. While everyone else was firmly in the twenty-first century, Tringle Nook was still struggling to catch up with the twentieth.

It was like living in a museum. Most of the residents weren't even on the Net. And, though Britain had long been a multi-cultural society, Tringle Nook simply hadn't noticed. It wasn't just Tringle Nook either. It was Cross Nook, Iggleby Tor, Rowanby, even Town. The whole area was fairly mono-culture. The locals still thought they were being ethnically daring if they had a Chinese take-away.

Anyway, Brad reflected, Tringle-Nookians were so old fashioned and insular they'd be unsettled by any incomer. Any 'townie', regardless of colour or creed. Incomers were regarded with suspicion. They had to prove themselves.

In the event, Sunil's family had no trouble settling. They were a great bunch. You couldn't help but like them and the locals soon came round. As for Brad, he'd been over the moon. A young family with three kids! Granted, two of them were three-year-old twin girls. But Sunil had been ten. His own age. A boy his own age, living just down the track!

'Hi,' said Sunil, as the boys met up where the tracks merged.

That's all that was said. Sometimes, they'd chatter all the way to the bus stop. At other times, they ambled along in silence. They were always in tune. They always knew whether it was a chatty day or a quiet day. Really good mates were like that, Brad thought. They knew.

The message was probably coming from him, today. He was shattered. He'd been up half the night playing 'Survival'. Making the most of the Blast-Pac, before he had to give it back. Playing in the dark, with the volume down, so his parents wouldn't suspect, had made the game more realistic than ever. It had been 4 a.m. before he'd been able to tear himself away.

He half glanced at Sunil whose dark skin was now as much a part of the local scenery as the sheep grazing in the fields. Not so when he'd first arrived, of course, when he'd been the very first non-white child in their tiny junior school. Their well-meaning teacher, Miss Wattle, had taken great pains to help him settle in. Amongst other things, she'd announced to the class that they were going to do a topic on India.

Sunil, like most new kids, had been dead quiet for the first couple of weeks, slowly taking everything in. The class had been warned off mentioning anything about race or culture, their natural curiosity squashed by grown-up political correctness.

'Perhaps Sunil can tell us something about where his family come from,' Miss Wattle ventured during week three.

'Er...' Sunil had said, glancing round nervously. 'Well it was different to here.'

'Yes, I expect so,' said Miss Wattle, encouragingly.

'There were more Asians.'

'Yes,' said Miss Wattle.

''Cos it was a big city and you got all sorts of different people, which was nice. But I like it here too,' Sunil added hastily.

'Good,' said Miss Wattle.

'I miss some things though,' said Sunil, relaxing a bit. 'Like the bowling alley, the shops and going to watch United on Saturdays.'

'Er...where exactly are we talking about, Sunil?'

'Manchester.'

'Ah,' said Miss Wattle, as light dawned. 'That's very interesting, Sunil. But I wasn't actually meaning where you were born. I meant do you know anything about where your family came from originally?'

'Oh!' said Sunil, brightly. 'Sorry. Yes. My dad came from North London and my mum was born in Cambridge. But her parents originally came from London, too.'

Miss Wattle gave up after that but she'd opened the floodgates. If it was all right for her to ask silly questions, then the class guessed they could do the same.

'What language do you speak at home, Sunil?'

'Welsh.'

'Does your mum wear one of them sari things?'

'Only for best, when she's sacrificing pigeons, every third Tuesday of the month.'

'Do you ever get sunburnt?'

'Only if I sit out after dark.'

It was that one which made people finally catch on. But they'd swallowed dozens of Sunil's outrageous answers before then.

'What are you laughing at?' Sunil said, as they reached the bus stop.

'You.'

'I haven't said anything.'

'Not now,' said Brad. 'When you were ten.'

Sunil didn't have time to question him. The bus had arrived early for once, and they made their way upstairs. There were very strict, unspoken rules on the bus. Seniors, from Year 10 like themselves, went upstairs but only the Upper Sixth were allowed in the back row. Juniors went downstairs. Most kids kept to the same places.

Brad and Sunil flopped down on their seat in front of Stacey and Steve Holton. The Holtons got on in town to be bussed out to Barnaby Merrick's because their parents hadn't been keen on the town school. It didn't have Merrick's reputation for music and the Holtons were all keen musicians.

Brad felt the crack on the back of his head almost as soon as he sat down.

'What's that for?' he asked, turning round and glaring at Stacey.

She flicked her blonde hair out of her eyes and glowered back at him.

'So where were you yesterday?'

'What?'

'You promised to come round.'

'I didn't,' said Brad. 'I said maybe, if I wasn't busy.'

'Look,' said Stacey. 'If you want us to finish, just say so, can't you? Instead of mucking me about all the time.'

'Do we have to have domestics on the bus, Stace?' said Steve.

'Shut it.'

Steve did as instructed. No-one argued with Stacey when she was throwing a moody.

'I don't want to finish,' Brad muttered, aware that half the bus was now listening.

He didn't either. Why should he? Stacey was one of the prettiest girls in the whole school. He'd liked her way back, when they were both in Year 7. But Merrick's was a big school. A good school with a reputation for music, sports and higher than average exam results. They took in kids from miles around. He and Stacey had never been in the same classes. Never really had a chance to get to know each other, until all the groups had been re-shuffled at the start of Year 10, in September, two months ago. They'd found themselves in the same sets for almost everything, got chatting and sort of drifted together.

OK, so it had been Stacey who'd made all the first moves. But Brad hadn't complained. He was one of the few lads in Year 10 to have a real girlfriend and all his mates were dead jealous.

Brad was thrown forward as the bus stopped. Last pick up before school. Cross Nook. The 'big' village, of all of thirty houses, where people from Tringle went to buy odd items from the local shop or to have a pint in The Bull. Only one person got on there. Colford was the only kid of senior school age who lived in Cross Nook. And he was Year 9 so, mercifully, stayed downstairs.

'So what kept you so busy, then,' Stacey was asking, 'that you couldn't even phone?'

'Dad needed a hand fixing the tractor.'

'All day?'

'Most of it, yeah.'

'Four o'clockish?'

'I reckon, yeah, why the inquisition?'

'Because I phoned at four o'clock and your Nick said you were nailed to that blasted machine of yours and he couldn't disturb you or you'd kill him. Apparently, he was supposed to tell me you were out.'

'Not you,' said Brad, almost wailing as Stacey tweaked his ear. 'That was the message if Colford phoned. I was gonna come round a bit later but I got carried away. Colford lent me this game and...'

'No!' said Stacey. 'Please. Don't bore me with your boys' toys.'

'They're not just for boys,' said Steve, forgetting to keep quiet.

'They're for people with one brain cell less than a dried pea,' said Stacey. 'So that sort of restricts it to lads, doesn't it?'

'Oh, come off it,' said Brad. 'They're not for dummies. You need concentration, strategy, good reflexes . . .'

'That's why girls don't like them,' said Steve. 'No co-ordination, see?'

'Either that or they're scared of damaging their nails on the control pad,' said Sunil.

'Who asked you?' Stacey snapped. 'Both of you. Butt out. I'm talking to Brad.'

It was too late. All the boys had warmed to the theme and gender wars continued for the rest of the journey. Stacey was undaunted by the fact that it was three against one, and the boys crawled off the bus with the uneasy feeling that Stacey, as usual, had won.

The school was what visitors termed 'imposing'. From the drive you could almost fancy yourself back in the eighteenth century, if you ignored the car park. Merrick Hall provided the central block of the school with its leaded windows and massive, oak doors. Only if you went round the back did you find signs of more modern architecture. The science and art blocks, added in the 1960s and recently renovated; the sports hall, drama studio and music rooms from the 1980s; and last year's brand new humanities block where Brad's class now registered.

At the front of the main building was the life-sized

statue of Barnaby Merrick, the man who'd once owned the Hall. As they passed, Brad put his arm round Stacey steering her away from the crowds, partly because he wanted to talk to her on his own and partly because he knew Colford wouldn't approach if he was with a girl. Colford, bless him, was still at that age where he blushed and stammered around girls. Especially girls like Stacey.

It wasn't so easy to avoid Colford at the end of the day. Stacey was staying on for orchestra. Normally Brad would have made a quick get-away but the bus was late. Apparently it had broken down and the company was trying to find a replacement. It was always happening. The few buses that were left were ages old. They had trouble getting the parts to fix them. Nobody except schoolkids used them much any more. How long would it be, Brad thought as he shuffled in what passed as a queue by the hall door, before the scenario in 'Survival' became horribly real? Not the massacres, but the decline of the towns, the cities, with more and more people shopping and working from home?

The trouble with thinking is that it makes you careless. Brad had forgotten to keep watch and, before he realized what was happening, a hunched figure had shuffled up beside him.

'Hi, Col,' said Brad, wearily. 'How's it going?'

'What?'

'Things. Life. School,' Brad explained.

Colford had a strangely literal view of the world. He wasn't thick, exactly. But you had to spell everything out for him. Jokes, for example, were a complete no-go area. Brad wouldn't even attempt a joke with Col.

'Oh, I see,' Col said. 'All right.'

Colford Rattersby was an incomer. Not quite as recent as Sunil but an incomer, none the less. His parents had moved into a run-down, not to say derelict, cottage in Cross Nook when Colford was a baby. The cottage was still a wreck. Colford and his dad were still there but Colford's mum had disappeared by the time he was four.

Brad didn't know the details. And, if anyone else did, they weren't letting on. Certainly not Colford. There was no evidence that he remembered he'd ever had a mum. Colford's dad hadn't let much slip either. Unlike Sunil's family, the Rattersbys had never quite fitted in.

Mrs Rattersby, apparently, had been very quiet. Kept herself very much to herself, before she suddenly took off. And Colford's dad didn't exactly mix either. He'd snarl hello, if you passed him on the river fishing, or out in the fields hunting rabbits with his dogs. He'd sometimes have a pint in The Bull. But mainly he had his own friends who he hung about with in town on Friday and Saturday nights. Nobody was quite sure what he did for a living, except that he went away a lot. And he always seemed to have plenty of money, though you'd never believe it, looking at the house.

'So when can I have my stuff back?' Colford was bleating. 'Have you got it?'

'Don't be daft. I wouldn't bring stuff like that into school,' said Brad.

'When then? Can I come round tonight?'

'No. I'm at footie training tonight,' Brad lied.

Once you let Col come round, you could never get rid of him.

'I'll bring them back tomorrow, after school, OK?'

Colford nodded, questioning him with those huge brown eyes. Trying to check whether he meant it. Looking at him, like the dogs did when they were begging for tit-bits. He reminded Brad of a dog. A spaniel, he decided. A floppy, soppy spaniel.

'Oi, Ratty,' a Year 9 lad yelled at Colford, before kicking a bag across the hall floor. 'This yours?'

People were getting bored. The bus still hadn't arrived and the duty teacher had wandered out to check. Big mistake. The queue had broken up completely. A scuffle had started between a couple of Year 11s at the back and now some of Colford's classmates were playing football with his bag.

Brad launched in for one of his famous tackles, intercepting the bag and following through to hack the leg of the lad who'd been kicking it. He picked up the bag and handed it to Colford.

The lad with the bruised leg scowled at them but did nothing. Brad was one of the larger Year 10s. Tall and with real muscle. Not generally aggressive but able to take care of himself. People knew not to mess with Lawrence Bradshaw.

'Thanks,' said Colford, beaming at him again.

Brad immediately regretted his heroics. He felt a bit

sorry for Colford. The way other kids picked on him. But he didn't want him to get the wrong idea. Like they were going to be big mates or anything.

Still, Brad thought, as the bus was announced and people started to surge forward. It might be worth something.

'Col,' he said, 'I couldn't keep the stuff till the end of the week, could I?'

'Couldn't you?' said Colford, misinterpreting as usual.

'I meant *can* I keep the stuff a bit longer?'

'Sure, Brad,' said Colford, as the queue came to a stop again, outside.

Brad stood on tiptoe, trying to see the cause of the hold-up. When he turned round, Colford was standing close to the black, marble statue of Barnaby Merrick, muttering to himself.

'What you doing, Col?' Brad asked.

'Talking to Mr Merrick,' said Colford, as if holding a conversation with a statue was the most natural thing in the world.

'Oh . . . right,' said Brad.

'He had a dead interesting life, you know,' said Colford, seriously. 'Bit sort of sad, really.'

'Yeah, I know,' said Brad. 'They never stop droning on about him in assemblies, do they? "Man who kept going in the face of all adversity . . . shining example to us all." Then there's the four-page history in the school prospectus, that Mum made me read when I joined the school.'

'I tried to read that,' said Colford. 'But it was all in

27

small print with loads of big words. So now I just talk to him. He's nice. He tells me things.'

'The statue tells you things?' said Brad.

He looked up at Merrick. Straight-backed, serious, almost military, though his clothes were civilian. Rather a gloomy figure to have looming over the school, Brad always thought. Chiselled lips, slightly down-turned, following the drooping line of the moustache. Deeply furrowed brow, etched over bushy eyebrows.

The eyes, Brad had to admit, were unusually expressive, for a statue. It struck him that they were very like Colford's eyes. Huge, sad, uncertain, questioning. But, apart from the eyes, the statue was as you might expect it to be. Still and definitely silent.

'Er... what sort of things does he tell you, Col?' Brad asked.

'Oh, just about his life and stuff,' said Col, casually, as people finally began to scramble onto the bus.

CHAPTER THREE

1895

Barnaby Merrick paced up and down the corridor, pausing every few minutes listening for tell-tale signs. Nothing. Ominous silence, broken only by the ticking of the grandfather clock. 3.15 p.m.

He strode towards the bedroom door, put his fingers on the handle, removed them and turned away. This was no place for him today. He would simply have to wait.

Wait as he'd done so many times before. The first time, seven years ago, the week before his twenty-first birthday. A double celebration had been planned for the birthday and for a far more important event. The anticipated arrival of his first-born child, barely a year after his marriage to Anne.

But congratulations had been premature. The child, a girl, had been still-born. He had turned away, unable to look, as Anne had cradled the lifeless body in her arms.

When Anne fell pregnant again, the doctor had advised total rest. She'd rested. She'd had the best possible care. Yet the child, Emily, had been frail. She'd lived only two weeks, but Barnaby could still trace every inch of her delicate features in his mind, feel her soft wisps of blonde hair beneath his fingers.

He turned to the window as cries shattered the silence. Not the cries he'd been expecting but boisterous, whooping, irritating squeals. Coming from outside. Burton, the gamekeeper, was striding across the lawn, his eldest lad, almost as tall, striding beside him. Hanging back, pushing and fighting, were two of his other boys, the two responsible for the noise. Three fine, sturdy, healthy lads, with their sisters, Ellen and Jane, back at the cottage helping Mrs Burton to look after baby Sam. Six children in all.

Why was it, Barnaby thought bitterly, that his workers bred so casually, so effortlessly, while he himself remained childless? Why did their children thrive whilst he watched his own wilt and fade?

His third child, Barnaby junior, had seemed strong and healthy enough, coming bawling and kicking into the world, almost killing his poor mother. Anne had been poorly for months afterwards. The doctor had muttered darkly that she simply wasn't strong enough to bear any more children.

It hadn't mattered. He didn't need any more. He wasn't a greedy man. One son would suffice. That was all he asked for. One son. He would have been happy with young Barnaby. He had been happy. Ecstatically happy, watching Barnaby crawl across the floor. Sitting him on the back of the grey pony, before he'd even taken his first steps. Hearing him say his first word, which had sounded, to his fond ears, like 'Papa'.

But Barnaby would never run about, shout, play like Burton's boys were doing. One night, he'd seemed quieter than usual. Listless. They'd sat up with him, watching. He became fretful, started burning up. They'd sent a servant for the doctor. They'd acted swiftly. They'd done everything right. But the fever had taken hold so quickly. Burnt so fierce.

Barnaby banged on the window, forcing the Burton lads to look up, stop their game and scurry off to join their father. He immediately felt mean, petty. It wasn't their fault. He didn't want them to look upon him as a fearsome ogre. He rather liked the lads. He liked all children.

He'd make a wonderful father, he was sure. He'd spent far more time with young Barnaby than was fashionably acceptable. Talking to him, telling him stories, carrying him round the grounds pointing out trees, birds, flowers, in that brief time they'd had together.

The grandfather clock struck four.

Time. Time. What use was time or money, when you were denied the one thing in the world that you wanted?

'Please God,' he cried out, as he heard his wife scream. 'Please God. This time.'

6.15. The light outside fading. Too long. Too long. His wife's cries. Maids running in and out. Doors banging. Anxious voices. Dogs barking. Everything but the sound he wanted to hear. The sound of a baby crying.

He couldn't bear it. He slumped onto the window seat, his head buried in his hands. He might have slept momentarily. He didn't know. He hadn't heard the bedroom door open. He hadn't been aware of any footsteps. He was aware only of the doctor's voice.

'Mr Merrick?'

Barnaby raised his head slowly, afraid to look. Then leapt to his feet, as he saw the doctor smile.

'Congratulations. You have a beautiful baby boy.'

'And Anne?'

'She's tired. Resting. I think she'll be fine but…'

No need to say more.

'You're my last hope, Charles Barnaby,' Mr Merrick whispered to his sleeping son, later. 'And nothing's going to take you from me. Please God.'

CHAPTER FOUR

Brad looked at his watch and started to jog down the lane. It was gone three o'clock already. How had he let Stacey hang onto him for so long? He hadn't wanted to spend his Saturday morning shopping in town at all. Who would? But after the bother the previous weekend, when he'd forgotten to go round, he guessed he'd better humour Stacey.

Halfway through the week, Stacey's best friend, Emma, had sidled up to Brad, dropping a less than subtle hint that Phil, in the Upper Sixth, had been hanging round Stacey.

'You know,' Emma had stressed, 'Phil with the red sports car.'

'And an ego the size of the solar system,' Brad had said. 'The one who dumps girls if they won't sleep with him on the first date . . . or even if they do! Nice try, Emma. But Stacey's not going to trade me for Philandering Phil!'

It had given him a jolt though. Stacey might not be daft enough to be taken in by Phil, but there were plenty of other lads around. Older lads. Emma's latest boyfriend was in the Lower Sixth. How long would it be before Stacey started looking for someone of similar status? So he'd agreed to the shopping trip, trailing round as Stacey blithely wandered from shop to shop. Sitting on hard chairs outside changing rooms while Stacey dived in and out.

'What d'yer reckon to these jeans, Brad?'

'Great.'

'No, they're not. They make me look fat.'

Too dangerous to agree. Almost as dangerous to disagree.

'Do you think the blue shirt or the white one? Brad, are you listening?'

'The white — No the blue,' he said, seeing the sneer which had greeted his first guess. 'The blue, definitely.'

'I think I'll try the black one.'

And so it had gone on. The clothes shops. The shoe shops. The make-up counter at Boots. Stacey liked to save her money up for one big blitz every so often. Things had looked a bit brighter when she'd decided to buy a CD. He'd almost got as far as looking at the games.

'Come on, Brad!' she'd said, clutching the small package.

For once, she'd known exactly what she wanted, and the transaction had taken less than a minute. The 'come on' hadn't, of course, meant they could go home. Stacey had informed him they were going to The Granary for lunch. No point pleading for the Burger Bar. Stacey was a health freak and a vegetarian. So Brad had tried to work up an appetite for the wholemeal sandwiches and gritty carrot cake which Stacey kindly treated him to.

He'd wolfed it down, desperate to get back for a go on 'Survival' before he had to help his dad with the milking. Suddenly the image of the empty city was extremely appealing. No shops! No shopping trips with fashion-crazed girlfriends. Imagine!

'Brad! You're not listening again,' she'd accused.

'Sorry. I was thinking.'

'Sleeping, more like. You look shattered. What've you been doing?'

'Shopping!'

'Rubbish! You were knackered when we set out.'

He didn't want to confess to Stacey that he'd been up every night till the early hours, playing the game.

'Yeah, well, shopping sort of finished me off,' he said, staring out of the window at the hordes of mindless zombies, clutching their glossy carrier bags.

'Can't think why people still do it,' he said. 'I mean, you can get everything now without ever leaving your sitting room but people don't, do they? They'd rather come into town to be trampled to death. I thought cities and towns were supposed to be under threat,' he added, wistfully.

'Only in your stupid games, dumbo,' said Stacey, leaning over to ruffle his hair. 'The analysts are way wrong about town centres. People are always going to want to come shopping. Trying things on, having a laugh with your mates, popping into the coffee bar. Screens are too impersonal. It takes all the fun out of shopping.'

Stacey's ideas of fun were clearly several light years removed from his own, Brad thought, pausing near the end of the lane to get his breath. He put his head down, feeling suddenly sick and dizzy. That grotty carrot cake, probably. Or was he getting unfit?

Maybe his mum and Stacey were right. Maybe he'd

been spending a bit too much time in front of a screen recently. Five hours or more, through each night. More than once he'd caught himself dozing off in school. And he hadn't bothered with football training last week. Or swimming club. Next week, he told himself, when he'd given the Pac and the game back to Colford. Then he'd catch up on his exercise and sleep.

He wondered whether Colford would notice if he kept them over the weekend. He was already a day later than promised. What difference could forty-eight hours make? He darted in, determined to go straight upstairs, but his mother had other ideas.

'Brad?' she yelled from the kitchen. 'Brad, is that you?'

Brad considered ignoring her but she had that 'I want to talk to you' tone, that couldn't be denied.

She had the 'I want to talk to you' look, as well. Brad hovered by the kitchen table, wondering what it was this time. His room was a mess and he'd left his dirty clothes on the bathroom floor. He hadn't done his homework yet. He'd rushed out without feeding the cats, which was his usual morning task. Maybe the footie coach had been on about him missing training again. It could be any number of things.

'Sit down.'

The voice was too sharp for the bathroom mess. Or the cats. That narrowed it down a bit.

'What's all this about some stuff of Colford's you've got?' she asked.

Nick, Brad thought. I'll kill him!

'That was last week,' he said. 'What's Nick told you?' he added, not wanting to confess to more than was strictly necessary.

'Nick hasn't told me anything. Mr Rattersby's been on the phone.'

'Oh.'

'You might well say "oh". I do not take kindly to having that man swearing down the phone at me. You know what he's like! He dragged up the bike business again and said if any of this stuff was damaged...'

'It's not,' said Brad. 'It's fine.'

'No, Brad,' said his mother. 'It is not fine. Poor Colford's going to be in dead trouble for lending it to you. His dad noticed it was missing this morning. It's the boy's birthday present, for heaven's sake.'

'I know,' said Brad. 'But he wasn't sure about setting it up and his dad's been away all this week, so I said I'd sort it for him.'

'All week?' said his mum. 'He's been away all week and left Colford on his own?'

'Yeah,' said Brad. 'He often does. Col's fourteen now, you know. He's not a kid.'

'I wouldn't leave you on your own for a week!'

Brad rolled his eyes. He'd be thrilled if his parents would leave him for half a day. But they never did. They were always around. Fussing. Making a big deal out of everything.

'So why couldn't you set it up at Colford's?'

'You don't let me go there!'

His parents didn't exactly ban him from the Rattersbys'. But it was true they didn't like him going there. They encouraged him to be nice to Colford. Colford, they felt sorry for. But they weren't sure about his dad. Or the three large dogs he kept.

'Yes, well,' said his mother. 'That's not the point. You know how we feel about you borrowing stuff from people without letting us know. Where is it, anyway?'

'In my room.'

'I couldn't find it,' she said. 'I went and looked after he phoned. Mind you, I'm surprised you can find anything under that rubble.'

Brad didn't tell her that he'd hidden it. He let her ramble on about the state of the room, the bathroom, the unfinished homework and the poor, starving cats he'd neglected. She managed to get in the full range of moans before finally returning to the original subject.

'Well you'd better go and get it then. Mr Rattersby's coming round at five. Bring it straight down.'

Brad did as instructed. No point arguing. The best he could hope for now was damage limitation. That his mother would be relieved that the stuff was going back. That she would show no further interest in the contents of the large carrier bag.

'Let's have a look,' she said. 'I didn't like the sound of what Mr Rattersby mentioned.'

An expression of horror settled on her face, as if Brad was unloading a pile of dead mice onto the kitchen table instead of a perfectly harmless jacket and game.

'Oh, Brad,' she said, examining 'Survival'. 'This looks awful. And what Mr Rattersby's doing buying a lad Colford's age one of those Blast jackets, I can't imagine!'

'They're good,' said Brad, defiantly.

'Wonderful,' she said. 'Killing. Being killed. What a pleasant way to spend your time. Well, I don't want you bringing stuff like this into the house again. What if Nick got hold of it?'

'No chance,' said Brad. 'He knows better than to muck with my stuff.'

'And that's another thing,' she said. 'He showed me that mark on his wrist where you grabbed him again the other day. And I'm not having it, Brad.'

'Sorry,' muttered Brad, knowing he'd gone a bit far with Nick.

'I wouldn't be surprised if it's these flaming games, making you all aggressive,' she said, staring at the box again before putting it back in the bag.

'Rubbish,' said Brad.

'It's not rubbish! I was watching a documentary about the effects of these violent games. A study showed that kids who played them were more likely to react aggressively, in certain situations, than those who didn't.'

'Yeah, but they're a fix, those studies, aren't they? The kids they used were probably violent to start with. I'm not.'

'Not usually,' said his mother. 'But I've noticed, this last month or so, how much you've been picking on poor Nick.'

Poor Nick. It was always poor Nick, Brad thought.

Mum didn't seem to notice what a pain he was. Never said a word when Nick was running round the house, screaming his head off, with Brad trying to do his homework. Never seemed to see when Nick was deliberately winding him up. But let him retaliate and Mum went wild. It wasn't just Mum either. Dad was as bad.

'Nick never moans when I ask him to help out,' Dad would say.

No matter that Nick made a muck-up of everything he touched, leaving gates open, cutting himself on tools or snarling up machinery.

'He's only young,' Dad would say. 'He tries.'

Brad didn't bother pointing any of this out to his mother. She wouldn't listen to his side of the story. She never did. Instead he simply shrugged and ambled out to help his dad. May as well notch up a few Brownie points before Mr Rattersby arrived and it started all over again.

Brad was still outside with Nick and his dad when Mr Rattersby strode up the lane with Colford trotting along behind him. Brad sent Nick in for the stuff and when he returned, Mum was with him. Obviously gearing up for a united front against Colford's dad.

'I'm sorry, Mr Rattersby,' said Brad, prompted by his mother's nudge, as she handed over the bag. 'But I've got the Pac set up and I've written out the main instructions for Col.'

'Have you now?' Mr Rattersby snarled. 'Well it better all be working. Or I'll be round again.'

That was it. Not another word. He just turned, pushed

Colford in front of him and strode off back down the lane. The Bradshaws all stared, silently, until they disappeared from view.

'Well,' said Mrs Bradshaw. 'That was short and sharp. I was going to ask if Colford wanted to stay for tea but I didn't get a chance!'

Brad tried not to look too pleased.

'Did you see those bruises under Col's eye and up his arms?' Mr Bradshaw mumbled. 'Honestly, that man wants locking up. I hope you realize, Brad,' he said more loudly, 'that you were probably responsible for that! That's why we tell you not to borrow stuff from Colford. His dad's hard enough on the lad, without you causing more hassle.'

Brad was about to argue, but changed his mind. The worst of it was, his dad was probably right. Mr Rattersby didn't need much of an excuse to hit Colford. Everyone in Tringle and Cross Nook knew it happened. The teachers at school knew. Social services knew. They'd been alerted more than once. Colford had his own social worker, a guy who turned up to see him at school sometimes. No point going to the house. Mr Rattersby would either pretend they weren't in or set the dogs loose.

Once, when Colford was at junior school, the police had been called in because Mr Rattersby had actually taken a swipe at the social worker and broken his nose. Colford had been taken into care for a few months but he'd run away and gone back to his dad.

It hadn't, Brad thought, been so bad recently. At junior school, the teachers had always been fussing over

Colford. Worried about him being withdrawn. Worried about his bruises. Worried about his strange outbursts. Colford, though generally quiet and placid, would erupt every now and again, throwing himself on the floor in a tantrum or chucking chairs around. Foster carers found him unmanageable.

Colford had spent short periods in three different foster homes that Brad knew about. But it never worked out. Col always went wild. Always absconded. For some crazy reason, he always went back to his dad.

The violence wasn't considered quite bad enough to force the issue and, mercifully, since Colford had been at Merrick's, there hadn't been so much trouble. Colford had settled quite well. Still quiet. Still a loner. Still picked on a bit by some of the yobs. But, as far as Brad knew, there hadn't been any furniture-throwing or behavioural problems, unless you counted talking to statues as a problem.

So mainly, these days, Col muddled along and was largely left to his own devices. There were kids at the school with far worse problems than Colford.

More importantly, you didn't see so much evidence of domestic aggro any more either, now that Colford was growing up. Until today. Brad hoped it was a one-off. That things would settle. But he promised himself he'd keep an eye on Colford, try to make it up to him a bit. And never, ever, would he borrow anything from him again.

CHAPTER FIVE

'I thought you liked "Ulti-Max",' Sunil complained, as Brad stared, listlessly, at the screen.

'I do,' said Brad who'd gone to considerable trouble to get it off Steve again and smuggle it into the house.

It was good. Very good. But the trouble was that without the Blast-Pac, nothing seemed particularly exciting any more.

It was almost two weeks since he'd given it back to Colford. Two dismally dull weeks. He'd got so desperate one night that he'd actually phoned Colford, checked that his dad wasn't in, and volunteered to go round. It had been a good evening. They'd played on 'Survival' for hours.

Actually, it had been Brad who'd played. Colford seemed more interested in droning on and on about the Merricks.

'Mr Merrick only had one child, you know, 'cos all the others died. Did you know that, Brad? That's why Mr Merrick loved Charles so much. He was a good dad. A proper dad. Like dads should be. He spent loads of time with Charles. Especially as Charles's mum was always so poorly. I mean, that must have been dead sad for Charles 'cos he never really got to know his mum. Like I never knew mine. But, in another way, Charles was lucky. Don't you think Charles was lucky, Brad? Having a dad like that? A dad who really cared about him. Don't you think so, Brad?'

Brad had largely ignored Colford. He'd ignored two phone calls from his parents, too, telling him it was time to come home. Brad had only finally bolted out of the back door when he'd heard Mr Rattersby returning. Mum and Dad hadn't been too pleased and had imposed a two-week pocket-money ban. But it had been worth it.

'If you're not going to enjoy anything without a Pac,' said Sunil, pausing the game, 'you'll have to get your parents to get you one for Christmas.'

'Tried that,' said Brad. 'I said I'd give up birthday and Christmas presents for the next three years, if they'd get me one. I even got our Nick to plead for one as a shared present. Bad move, that. Mum went hysterical, accusing me of corrupting the poor little dear! Even if we had the money, they wouldn't buy me one.'

'My dad's the same,' said Sunil, somewhat unnecessarily.

Sunil didn't even have his own machine. The family had an ancient shared PC and an old 2D games console. That was it. Almost techno-phobic.

Brad turned his attention back to 'Ulti-Max'. It was definitely one of the better games. As soon as he'd saved up enough money, he was going to buy it for himself, no matter what Mum said. It would be even better if you had a Game-Scan but there was no chance of one of those appearing in his Christmas stocking.

Brad tried instead to use his imagination to pep the game up a bit. To imagine familiar features, instead of the rather bland figure on the screen, whom he was supposed to be stalking. He tried thinking of his maths teacher, who'd given him a detention for not doing his home-work. His first detention, ever! Totally out of order. The homework was done. He'd simply left it at home. Twice. When he'd been too tired to think straight, after he'd been playing 'Survival'.

Easy enough to imagine Mr Smart, with his fuzzy ginger hair and beard, but the image didn't last long. Brad tried instead that Year 9 kid who'd made him mad, yesterday, when he'd caught him taking money from Colford in the playground.

'Taking' might have been a bit of an exaggeration. Colford had quite clearly been offering the money, willingly. He did things like that sometimes, but it didn't mean people should take advantage. Still, angry as Brad had been, he couldn't remember the kid that well now. And his imagination simply wasn't that strong.

Either that, or he didn't hate anyone enough to place them in the game. So maybe a Game-Scan would be a waste of money. He couldn't even see himself scanning Nick's obnoxious face in. It would be a bit creepy, stalking someone you knew. Maybe Stacey was right.

'You'd have to be a psycho in the first place to want one of those things,' she'd said during one of their many arguments about techno-games.

The trouble with Stacey was she had a bit of a jealous nature.

'You think more of that rotten games machine than you do of me,' was one of her more familiar complaints.

And when she'd seen him talking to Tanya in the

dinner queue, she'd cornered him later and belted him across the face. Talk about double standards. She was the one who was always going on about male violence!

'Prat!' Sunil suddenly yelled. 'You've been spotted. You're not concentrating, Brad.'

Concentration wasn't usually one of Brad's problems. Never had been. He'd always been able to keep his head down at school and focus on what he was doing, even in their open-plan junior school where there were always dozens of people milling around and you had to do your sums with the infants singing 'Five little ducks went swimming one day' at the tops of their squeaky little voices.

'Couldn't someone shoot those flaming ducks?' Eddie Scott would whine, while Sunil would forget all about his sums and start singing along.

Sunil had found the open-plan school difficult to cope with. His old junior school had been traditional, with boxed-in sound-proof classrooms. He blamed the five little ducks for the fact that he was now only in Set 3 for maths. He was in top sets for most subjects, but only in a few did he and Brad find themselves together. English was one where Brad, Sunil, Stacey and Emma sat together in a foursome.

English was one of Brad's favourite subjects. He enjoyed reading the novels, plays or poems, having discussions or even writing. The teacher, Mrs Deale, was brilliant, if a little old fashioned.

So on Tuesday morning Brad slipped 'Ulti-Max' into Stacey's bag for her to give to her brother, and settled down, prepared for action. Until Mrs Deale uttered the dreaded word: 'Comprehension'.

Brad hated comprehension. He could never see the point. It was all so painfully obvious. Read a couple of passages. Answer questions. The answers were all in there. All you had to do was look. Easy!

Not so for most of the class, unfortunately. Even some of the brighter ones seemed to struggle. Mrs Deale would insist on reading it through together, before going over it all again, discussing, analysing every line, every comma, every metaphor.

The passages were apparently chosen for their very dullness, defying even Mrs Deale to inject any interest value.

'Hey, this is good,' said Stacey, the minute the papers landed on the desk. 'Check this out, Brad.'

It was always print-outs in English lessons. Mrs Deale was a techno-phobe who wouldn't let them work directly from screens.

Brad frowned as his eyes scanned the first page. The frown deepened as he flipped over to the second page and the third. Not as dull as usual, granted, but decidedly irritating. Especially with Stacey sitting there, gloating.

'This is rubbish,' he announced to anyone who was listening. 'It's completely unbalanced. Both articles are saying the same thing.'

'While I can't help being impressed that you've managed to analyse both passages so thoroughly in the space of thirty seconds,' said Mrs Deale, 'I really feel it would be better if you reserved your opinion until we'd read them through, Brad. You'll be able to state your case when you answer the questions.'

Dead right, Brad thought, sitting back, as Mrs Deale asked Sunil to read aloud. The first passage was an article taken from a Sunday newspaper, with the headline 'Deadly Games'. Subtitled: 'Are these games damaging your children?'

And guess what? The paper had decided they were.

Sunil stopped reading after the first couple of lines.

'Yeah,' he said. 'But nearly everyone plays the games and we don't all go around shooting people, do we?'

'Hopefully not,' said Mrs Deale, dryly. 'And that will certainly be a point for discussion later, but if you could just stick to the text for the moment, Sunil, please.'

'"The Home Secretary has called for greater censorship,"' Sunil dutifully read on.

Brad rolled his eyes and pulled faces at the boy opposite. This drivel just wasn't worth listening to.

'Thank you, Sunil. Could you continue, please, Brad?' said Mrs Deale.

Brad flashed Stacey a grateful smile as she pointed out where they were up to but the smile faded as he started to read. Especially when he got to the bit which was calling for a ban on the new Blast-Pacs and Game-Scans.

Evidently most of the class felt the same way, as everyone started shouting the minute he finished reading.

'It's nice to see you all so enthusiastic, for once,' Mrs Deale informed them. 'But I think we'll save discussion until we've read both pieces.'

The second article was a study by psychology students at an American university. They'd taken two groups of teenagers, giving one group nice, peaceful games to play, whilst the other group were given shooting games. After playing, both groups were given a set of pictures to comment on.

Brad looked at a copy of one of the pictures: an old lady in a narrow alley. Two lads, one of them taking the woman's shopping bag.

And surprise, surprise, thought Brad, as Emma read the accompanying text. The kids who'd played the peaceful games said the boys in the picture were helpful little Boy Scouts or something and those who'd played the violent games reckoned the woman was being mugged! Sounded exactly like the survey his mother had been telling him about.

'What a load of rubbish,' Brad said, the minute Mrs Deale invited comment. 'I play loads of games and they don't affect what I think or how I act.'

'Maybe the games don't influence you, Brad,' one of the girls interrupted. 'But the point is, they influence *some* people.'

Comments bounced all round the room. One, in particular, stood out.

'Brad's wrong,' Stacey claimed. 'He *is* influenced by them. He's like a flaming zombie when he's been on that machine.'

'Let's not make it personal, Stacey,' said Mrs Deale, before Brad could defend himself.

'Yeah, but Stacey's right,' said Emma. 'It's a boy thing, isn't it? It's all they ever talk about. It brings out their natural, brainless aggression, doesn't it?'

Neanderthal snarls and grunts from most of the boys.

'It's not just a boy thing,' said Paula, as the bell rang for break. 'I play "Burn Out" and "Mayhem" and stuff.'

That little confession, Brad thought as they left the classroom, rather served to confirm what the articles were saying. Paula was forever in trouble for her confrontational behaviour.

He tried to ignore the smirk on Stacey's face as they wandered outside with Sunil and Emma. Emma led the way, ambling with intent towards the sixth-form block, hoping to catch sight of the latest object of her affections.

They didn't actually get that far though. Just round the corner, slouching against the wall, was Colford, with his arm held up to his nose and the sleeve of his pale jacket slowly turning red.

'What's happened to you, Col?' said Emma, immediately going into mother-hen mode. 'Here, have a tissue.'

It was a big school but everyone knew Colford. Funny how you could be dead quiet and still manage to stand out, Brad thought, as Stacey put her arm round Colford, whose cheeks immediately flared as red as his blood-soaked sleeve.

'Come on,' said Stacey. 'I'll take you to the medical room.'

'No!'

'Leave him,' said Sunil. 'He'll be OK in a minute. It's stopped bleeding, I think. Did someone have a go at you?'

'It wasn't that kid from the other day again, was it?' said Brad.

Colford shook his head.

'Who then?'

'No-one. It just happened.'

'Did that bruise just happen on its own too?' said Emma.

Sunil shot her a warning glance. Brad had told him where Colford's latest bruises had come from.

'It was Derek Pomfritt who hit him,' said a junior girl, who'd been hovering with her friend. 'We saw it.'

Brad and his friends couldn't help smiling. Derek was another kid everyone knew. Only Year 7. Smallest kid in the school. Fast, nippy, like a terrier. But fairly ineffectual. Usually got picked on himself. Not exactly what you'd call dangerous.

'I hope you thumped him back, Col,' said Stacey.

'I thought you didn't believe in violence,' said Sunil.

'That's not violence,' said Stacey. 'That's defending yourself. That's different.'

'I'll sort Derek out,' said Brad, sure that Colford hadn't stood up for himself.

'Don't you go hitting him!' said Stacey.

'Geroff,' said Brad. 'What d'yer take me for? I'm not going to thump some pathetic Year 7 – no matter how many video games I play. I'll just warn him off Col, that's all.'

The liquid brown eyes stared at him again, in silent admiration. Playing hero to Colford was getting to be a

50

bit of a habit. He'd have to pack it in, Brad thought, as he walked off to find Derek.

He'd just turned the corner, by the statue, when he stopped, aware of footsteps behind him.

'You don't have to come with me, Col,' he explained. 'It'll be better if I just have a quiet word with him on my own.'

'I'm not coming with you,' said Colford. 'I'm going to talk to Mr Merrick. He likes me to tell him about any bother.'

'Does he?'

'Yeah,' said Colford. 'Mr Merrick understands because he went to boarding school when he was a boy, and he used to get beaten by the teachers and prefects. With a thick cane or a strap! It was supposed to toughen you up, Mr Merrick says. Make a man of you. But Mr Merrick doesn't believe in hitting kids.'

Brad wondered where Colford was getting his information from. Or whether he was simply making it up. He wondered whether he ought to try to put a stop to it. Surely it couldn't be good for Col to keep fantasizing like this?

On the other hand, maybe it was OK. Lots of kids had imaginary friends, didn't they? His brother Nick had once befriended an invisible polar bear and every night, for three months, Nick had badgered Mum into cooking two fish fingers for its tea!

Mum had said it was best to play along. That the bear would leave in its own good time. And it had. The day Nick started nursery.

So, all right, Col wasn't a toddler and maybe he was a bit old for that sort of stuff. But, like with the invisible polar bear, it was probably best to accept it. After all, what harm could it do?

'Mr Merrick tells me about all the rotten things that happened to him,' Colford was confiding. 'When he was a lad and when he was grown up. So that sort of cheers me up. Knowing that a bloke like him had problems too.'

'Great,' said Brad, pleased that Col's little game was at least helpful. 'Whatever works for you, Col.'

CHAPTER SIX

1900

Barnaby Merrick stood on the steps, shielding his eyes from the glare of the July sun. It was the sun which had made them water, he told himself. Nothing else. He wasn't crying. He hadn't cried since he was eight years old and his spaniel pup, Roly, had died after being trampled by a horse.

'Big boys like you don't cry,' his father had told him firmly. 'Come on. Dry those eyes. We'll get you another puppy.'

Some things were easily replaceable, Barnaby told himself, as he walked down the steps. Others weren't. But he hadn't cried when little Emily had died. Nor even when he'd lost Barnaby junior. What good, after all, did crying do?

At the bottom of the steps he stopped, shifting himself into a more comfortable position, away from the glare. Waiting until his eyes stopped watering. Quietly watching the scene on the far lawn. Nanny and one of the younger maids were sitting on a blanket under a tree, with a picnic spread out in front of them. It looked appetizing enough but the two young boys with them weren't interested in food. They were busy playing.

Charles was picking up his toy drum and bugle. He looked at them carefully, before deciding which one to give to Sam Burton, the gamekeeper's youngest lad. He handed Sam the drum, then took it back. He handed him the bugle whilst he put the drum strap round his own neck. Then he took the bugle back too, attempting to play both as they started to march.

Barnaby felt a faint smile creep across his lips as he edged forward, hoping to catch some of the conversation which was muffled by the tinny beat of the drum.

'All right, Sam,' Charles said as the bugle fell from his mouth onto the grass. 'You may have the bugle. But you must march behind me. Not next to me, like that,' he added pushing Sam out of the way.

'Why?' said Sam.

'Because I'm the General and you're only a common soldier,' Charles told him.

That's my boy, Barnaby Merrick thought. A born leader. Charles showed great promise. If only he could stay well. Both he and Sam were five years old, yet Sam was at least a head taller, stocky and solid, where Charles was thin and bony. Young Sam had never had a day's illness in his life whilst poor Charles seemed to succumb to everything. However much they nurtured and protected him, he still got sick.

'But he recovers,' the doctor had said. 'That's the thing! He's got a real inner strength, that lad of yours. A will to live. A survival instinct. He'll be fine. You'll see.'

Maybe the doctor was right, Barnaby thought, as the boys abandoned their music and started to roll around on the lawn. Charles did seem to be getting stronger.

'Let him out more in the fresh air, if I may suggest, sir,' Burton had urged at the start of last summer. 'It doesn't do to keep them cooped up inside, sir.'

Charles rolled away from Sam and picked up a stick from beside the tree.

'Now I've got a gun,' he announced. 'So you can be the

54

enemy. And I'll shoot you. Bang. Bang. No! Don't fall down, Sam. I missed. I haven't killed you yet.'

Little Sam stood up again. Barnaby had come out specially to talk to Charles but the boys were having such fun, the time didn't seem right. He wouldn't spoil their game. There would be time enough for sadness. The news would wait.

'BANG. BANG. Now you're dead! Now you fall down, Sam. Don't laugh! You don't laugh when you're dead. Do you, Nanny?'

Nanny was still chatting, so Charles swung round wildly, looking for someone else to confirm his view. He spotted his father before Barnaby could withdraw.

Charles raced over and threw himself at Barnaby, poor Sam quite abandoned.

'I'm a soldier today,' he announced, as his father picked him up. 'And I've just killed Sam. But he won't die properly. So that's not fair, is it? People should die properly, shouldn't they?'

Barnaby blinked, his eyes still sore from the sun.

'How's Mama?' Charles suddenly asked. 'Is she better? Can I see her?'

'So, you're a soldier today?' said Barnaby, putting his son on the ground and kneeling beside him. 'Good. That's good. Because soldiers, you know, are very brave. Soldiers don't cry, even when very sad things happen. Do they?'

'I expect not,' said Charles.

'So you mustn't cry either, Charles. What I've got to tell you is very sad. But you mustn't cry. Mama wouldn't have wanted you to cry...'

CHAPTER SEVEN

Brad's English lesson, at the end of the week, resumed where they'd left off. The discussion about the possible effect of video games became increasingly rowdy, until Mrs Deale announced she was getting a headache and it was time to do some writing. In silence.

Brad raced through the first twenty, painfully simple questions, requiring you to pick out answers from the text. The next section was a bit trickier, asking you to analyse how the writer in each case managed to get their point across. But they'd done similar exercises before. 'Persuasive' writing. Tricks used by advertisers, politicians, campaigners and journalists to make you see their point of view.

In this case, they hadn't succeeded with Brad, and he launched into Task 3 with enthusiasm. Writing either in support of, or against, the idea that violent video games contributed to crime and should be banned.

They'd been told to finish it for homework, finding as much information and evidence in support of their argument as possible. Brad had searched the Net, finding numerous studies and reports condemning the games and not so many in support of his own stance that this was all hysterical nonsense, perpetrated by ageing techno-phobes who simply didn't understand. Still, drawing on the information and personal experience, he'd managed to back up his point quite effectively, he felt.

The problem was whether to bother writing it up to his usual high standard or just to dash off a couple of paragraphs. It was a real dilemma. He was interested in the topic, felt almost driven to put the 'pro-games' viewpoint as strongly as possible, but there was a danger.

Mrs Deale had reminded them that it was coming up to their turn in the Debating Society rota. Debates took place once a fortnight, in the main hall. For each debate there were four speakers, two on each side. Classes from Year 9 upward took it in turns to provide speakers.

Anyone could attend the debates. Juniors were particularly encouraged to go along to see how it was done, so they'd be more likely to volunteer to speak, when they were older.

Brad had attended hundreds of debates in his time. But it hadn't encouraged him in the slightest and so far he'd managed to avoid speaking. There were always enough extroverts keen to volunteer. It wasn't that Brad was shy. Far from it. He had no trouble chatting to people or answering in class. But the thought of standing up in front of a big audience terrified him.

It was stupid, irrational, like all phobias, but Brad honestly thought he'd rather be nailed to a spit and roasted alive. So Mrs Deale's announcement that video games were to be the topic for their debate and that she'd be picking the four pupils who wrote the best arguments to speak in it had somewhat dampened Brad's enthusiasm for the weekend homework.

It had quite the opposite effect on most people. Even the kids who didn't like writing too much had darted off, determined to make an effort, desperate for their moment of glory in the hall. Sunil and Stacey were regular speakers. Full of themselves, the pair of them. You'd think they'd be dead certs to be chosen except Mrs Deale had added, ominously, that she was on the lookout for people who hadn't yet had a go.

Memories of this warning clinched the matter. Brad restricted himself to a few main points and turned to his maths. That, at least, was safe. No-one was going to ask him to give a talk on simultaneous equations. He abandoned the equations half an hour later when Sunil came round, hopefully clutching his football.

'Go and see if Nick wants to play,' said Brad. 'And I'll give Col a ring, so we can have two against two.'

'We are in a good mood today,' said Sunil, amazed that Brad should suggest including the two people he usually tried hardest to avoid. Brad smiled and went off to make the phone call.

'Yeah, Col. "Survival" and the Pac, if you can.'

'Hang on,' said Sunil, hearing the end of the call. 'I thought we were playing footie.'

'We are. But it looks like it might rain. Or we might get fed up.'

'You will, you mean,' said Sunil. 'Honestly, Brad. Stacey's right. You're becoming a fanatic. It's all you want to do, these days.'

'Rubbish.'

'Anyway, I thought you weren't supposed to borrow Col's stuff.'

'I'm not borrowing it. He's bringing it and he's going to take it back home again. That's not borrowing.'

And Sunil was wrong, Brad decided later, as he lay in bed, going over the events of the day. He wasn't a fanatic. Sure, he'd given up on the football after five minutes. But who wouldn't under the circumstances? The field was like a swamp. Col was useless and Nick was worse, whining every time you tackled him. Sunil sided with Nick, claiming fouls every two seconds.

They were best left to it, playing on their own while he went inside with 'Survival'. He'd almost completed level four but he wasn't a fanatic. He'd proved it. As soon as it got dark, as soon as Colford had to leave, he'd given the stuff back. Not easy, especially with Colford pressing him to keep it overnight, because his dad would be out and come home so late and so drunk that he wouldn't notice. Tempting. But Brad had refused, putting the memories of what had happened last time before his own, selfish instincts. Determined, too, to keep his promise to Stacey. He'd said he'd go round and he had.

A bit of a waste of time, admittedly. Girls were never satisfied. You could never please them. The evening had started off well enough. Steve and Stacey, who got on remarkably well for brother and sister, had invited a few mates round, made some pasta, put some music on and handed round cans of beer. Not a party, exactly. More of a party-planning session. It was the first week of December and they were gearing up for Christmas, deciding who was going to do what, with whom and where.

No point volunteering his house for revelry. The most his parents would allow, by way of alcohol, was a daring apple juice-based punch, with a splash of wine and tons of disgusting fruit.

Emma's parents were known to be quite liberal with the booze but they insisted on staying in, poking their noses round the door every thirty seconds in case anybody was getting carried away and actually daring to enjoy themselves. Paula's mum was dead fussy, but they'd had good parties round her dad's place more than once. So that was provisionally booked for the first venue, on the evening they broke up from school.

It hadn't taken long to get the rest sorted out. It was always the same people who had the parties. The girls, as always, did the organizing, debating deeply important issues like who was to provide the crisps and whether they were going to have a theme. Girls couldn't just party. Half the fun was the organization. Being bossy. Doing what they did best.

Was it any wonder that some of the lads got a bit bored, slowly drifting off up to Steve's room to try out his latest game? OK for the bachelor bunch, the ones the girls hadn't yet got their claws into. Brad had only managed to escape for five minutes before Stacey had burst in, claiming he'd been gone for hours. They'd had a bit of a row. Well, quite a lot of a row, Brad acknowledged, as he lay in the dark, trying to put it out of his head, desperate to get some sleep.

He'd stormed out in the end and phoned Dad to pick him up. But Dad had taken ages and Brad had stood outside in the freezing rain, rather than listen to any more of Stacey's lecturing.

Did it mean they were finished? Was it any worse than their previous rows? Would he end up grovelling, like he usually did? Probably. He wasn't quite sure why but Stacey had sort of got to him. She was his first girlfriend unless you counted Hannah Morris who he'd kissed twice when they were in Infants. Or Tanya who he'd had a brief fling with, when he'd first started to notice girls back in Year 7. As the fling had consisted of holding hands once or twice in the corner of the playground, he didn't think it counted. Teased by their friends, they'd soon given up thoughts of romance. Hormones had been put on hold. Brad had drifted back to his first love, games, and he and Tanya had gone back to being friends.

Their friendship had gone undercover since he'd been going with Stacey. Stacey didn't approve of him hanging round other girls. Stacey didn't approve of much, he thought bitterly. She was always trying to change him. So why bother? Let her come chasing after him, if she wanted to. Having a girlfriend was OK. Good for his image and all that, but it certainly wasn't worth all this hassle. He looked at the clock. Almost midnight. Was it too late to phone her?

He switched on the bedside light and got out of bed, hovering by the desk. What he needed was a distraction. Something to stop his feet from moving. Something to stop his hands reaching for that phone. He moved quickly across the room and started sorting through his games. 'Carnage' – he hadn't played that for a while.

He was still playing an hour later when the house erupted. First the doorbell, then both dogs barking, Nick yelling for Mum, bedroom doors slamming. Brad quickly switched off his machine and followed the rest of the family downstairs.

Stacey? It couldn't be Stacey. You wouldn't catch Stacey apologizing, full stop! Let alone coming round at this time. Who then? Who on earth would come visiting at one o'clock in the morning? One thing was for sure, it wouldn't be good news.

It wasn't. As he reached the door, his mother was pulling something in from outside. A soaking wet, bedraggled something. A something wearing pyjamas with a green cagoule thrown over the top and a pair of large, black wellies.

'Col!' Brad exclaimed. 'What on earth are you doing?'

'The ceiling's leaking,' Colford mumbled.

'Sorry?' said Mrs Bradshaw.

'Yes,' said Colford, forlornly. 'I'm sorry to trouble you.'

'Ceiling?' said Brad, as his mother steered Colford into the kitchen, next to the Aga to get warm. 'Which ceiling? What do you mean?'

'I was having this dream,' said Colford, apparently ignoring the question. 'About living at Merrick Hall. In the old days. I was out shooting with Mr Merrick and suddenly it started to rain. I was all soaked and shivering.

62

Only it wasn't a dream any more. There was water pouring onto my bed from this big hole in the ceiling. And I didn't know what to do.'

'And I take it your dad's not at home?' said Mrs Bradshaw.

'No,' said Colford. 'He hasn't come in. I don't know where he is. I'm sorry! I didn't know what to do!'

Nobody asked why Colford hadn't simply phoned or why he had walked all the way to Tringle rather than wake one of his neighbours. Colford didn't always do the obvious and besides, his father had never exactly encouraged neighbourliness. He'd fallen out with most of the people in Cross Nook over the years.

'So how bad is it?' Mr Bradshaw asked.

'It's very wet,' said Colford.

'I'd better go and take a quick look then. You'll have to come back with me to let me in and keep the dogs off,' Mr Bradshaw added.

'The dogs are tied up,' said Colford, pleadingly. 'And I can give you the keys.'

'Good,' said Brad's mum. 'Because there's no way you're going out again. Look at him! He's shivering. Nick, go and get some of Brad's clothes for poor Colford. Brad, you can get dressed and go with your dad.'

'Do I have to?' Brad yawned.

Nobody said anything. The looks were enough. He had to go out in a near gale, stand in a cold room, plugging up a hole in Colford's ceiling whilst Col sat drinking hot chocolate by their Aga, wearing Brad's

63

clothes, being fussed over by Brad's mum. Wonderful!

'Not a lot we can do tonight,' Mr Bradshaw said, as they stood in Colford's room watching an ever-growing damp patch leaking water onto the bed. 'I'll move the furniture. Maybe stuff a sheet into that hole. You go downstairs, see if you can find any buckets.'

Brad moved as quietly as he could, not wanting to upset the dogs any further. They were chained up outside, barking and howling. Not the sort of excitable warning yap his own dogs made. These dogs meant business. If they were to get loose, they'd tear you apart. He managed to find a bucket and a large bowl amongst the rubble at the back of the cottage. Upstairs, his dad had moved the bed and one or two other bits out of the way.

'Do you think I should leave a note to tell Mr Rattersby where Col is?' Brad said.

He had to repeat the question because his dad couldn't hear properly above the sound of the rain and the dogs.

While his dad manoeuvred the bucket into place, Brad took a pen and scrap of paper out of Colford's school bag and perched on the window ledge to write. Colford didn't have a desk, table or chair in his room. Nothing much of anything, really. Not even a carpet. Just an old rug thrown over rough, bare floorboards.

Brad had never been in Colford's room before. On the few occasions he'd been round, they'd stayed in the sitting room. Possibly the only decent room in the cottage, it was dominated by the very latest Home Entertainment

Unit on which Colford watched films, listened to music, accessed the Net and played his many games. Brad wouldn't want to swap his life for Colford's but you had to envy his flash toys.

As Brad finished the note, he looked up, knowing something was wrong. A subconscious instinct for trouble, sharpened by playing the games. An instinct which allowed you to filter information, even when you weren't looking for it. The awareness of the silence, where the barking of the dogs had once been. The knowledge that someone was watching you.

His dad's reflexes were slower by far. He was still mucking about with the bucket and bowl. He didn't for the moment see what Brad saw. The figure of Mr Rattersby standing in the doorway, his bulging eyes bloodshot, his greying hair wild and windswept.

Brad had faced this scene many times in his games. But there was no comparison. Anyone who thought you could confuse games and reality was an idiot. The sensation of adrenaline-fuelled excitement he felt when facing a techno shoot-out was nothing like the ice-cold terror which now gripped him, faced with Mr Rattersby's shotgun.

CHAPTER EIGHT

1905

The shot rang out, echoing round the woods.

'Good lad, Charles,' said his father, as they both hurried forward.

Ten-year-old Charles looked down at the brightly coloured feathers of the bird at his feet. Its cold beauty, its stillness stirred memories.

'You're getting to be a fine shot,' said Mr Merrick, proudly.

The boy was coming on, no doubt about it. He was taller than Burton's lad, Sam, now and, though Charles was still slender, he'd lost that early, worrying sickliness.

'Those that fall prey to illness when they're babies,' Nanny had said, 'often turn out the strongest.'

He was clever too, Barnaby thought. Charles had turned out to be all that he'd ever wanted in a son. It was sad that Anne hadn't lived to see him growing up. And maybe, he acknowledged, it was bad for the boy, being brought up without a mother.

Barnaby had thought about re-marrying once or twice over the last five years. He wasn't yet forty. Passingly handsome and wealthy enough to be a fair catch, he had attracted plenty of interest. But, somehow, none of them could compare with Anne. And he and Charles seemed to get along so well together, it had seemed a shame to spoil it. If he were being honest with himself, he thought, he didn't want to share Charles with anyone.

'Mama's in heaven, isn't she?' said Charles suddenly, breaking into his father's thoughts.

'Yes,' said Barnaby, used to answering such questions which cropped up spasmodically over the years.

'But not everyone goes to heaven when they die?'

'Only the good people,' Barnaby confirmed.

'And what about this bird?' said Charles. 'Will it go to heaven... if it's been a good bird?'

'No, of course not!' said Barnaby, laughing.

'Why not?'

'Because it's only a bird.'

'But God made the birds, didn't he?'

'You know He did.'

'So why doesn't He care about them?'

'He does. It's just that...'

Charles needed to go to school, Barnaby thought. He had tutors, of course, but it wasn't the same. He needed to get out into the world, broaden his outlook, find other people to answer his questions.

The trouble was, Barnaby had such dreadful memories of his own school days, it wasn't the sort of thing he wanted to inflict on Charles. Besides which, he simply couldn't bear to part with him.

'It's just that animals are different from people,' Barnaby continued. 'They don't have souls.'

'I see,' said Charles, raising his gun, taking aim and firing again.

'Better make that the last,' said Barnaby, looking at the sky. 'We're a fair way from home and it's just starting to rain.'

Not that Barnaby cared about a few drops of rain, but he wasn't going to risk Charles getting soaked through and catching a chill. Chills could be dangerous. Charles might be getting stronger but there was no way Barnaby was taking any chances.

CHAPTER NINE

It was OK, Brad told himself, trying to breathe calmly, trying not to make eye contact with Mr Rattersby. Mr Rattersby thought they were burglars. Coming home, finding the door unlocked, hearing people moving about the house. It was an easy mistake to make. He was only protecting himself and his property. Any second now, he would recognize them. Put the gun down. Just keep calm. Keep calm.

'What the .. ?'

Mr Bradshaw had finally noticed what was going on and, in an attempt to stand up, had knocked over the bucket which clattered onto the bare floorboards. Mr Rattersby raised the shotgun slightly.

He must have recognized them by now, Brad thought. There was no light on in the room. They'd thought it too dangerous with the water leaking so close to the flex. But the hall light was on. It was clear enough to see.

'It's all right,' Mr Bradshaw was saying, in what was supposed to be a reassuring voice. 'It's me, Gordon Bradshaw. And Brad, Colford's friend. The ceiling's leaking.'

'Where's Colford?' Mr Rattersby snarled.

'He's at our house,' said Brad. 'Getting dried out.'

'Oh,' said Mr Rattersby, as though he barely believed them.

He swayed slightly, but Brad was relieved to see the gun being lowered.

'I'll bring him back in the morning,' said Mr Bradshaw. 'If that's all right with you.'

'I suppose it'll have to be,' snapped Mr Rattersby.

Brad cringed as Mr Rattersby stepped forward but he seemed to have lost all interest in them, collapsing onto the damp bed. Seconds later, he was snoring.

'Well!' said Mr Bradshaw, as they made their way out. 'I don't think I'll bother going back there for a while.'

Every cloud has a silver lining, or so his granddad used to say, Brad reflected, as he put the finishing touches to his homework the following Friday evening. And perhaps Granddad had been right. There'd been two definite silver linings this week.

The first was on Monday. The worry about how to approach Stacey, what to say to her, had completely evaporated, thanks to Mr Rattersby. The events of the early hours of Sunday morning provided the perfect talking point on the bus. Or rather whispering point. Brad had taken care to ensure that only Sunil and the Holtons heard him. He didn't want the story to get round. They hadn't told Colford about his father's belligerence, had made no mention of being threatened with a shotgun.

'No point upsetting the lad,' Mr Bradshaw said. 'He's a bundle of nerves, as it is. And, after all, there was no harm done.'

No harm but just enough threat of it to turn it into a cracking story, with only the slightest exaggeration.

Stacey had been horrified that Mr Rattersby even had a gun. She was a real townie, was Stacey. Very anti-blood sports. Didn't eat meat. Was always the first to volunteer for any debates involving animal rights. 'This house believes that animal organs belong in animals, not people' and 'This house believes there are animals in heaven' were two she'd managed to win. Not bad in a country school where most kids had been brought up with a less sentimental view of animals.

And Brad would never forget the day she'd laid into Eddie Scott for killing a wasp! She was a great one for over-reacting, was Stacey.

'You should have gone to the police!' she'd informed Brad, when he got to the end of his Mr Rattersby story.

'Nothing much they could do,' said Brad. 'It would have just caused a fuss and a load of aggro for Col, probably.'

'But he could have killed you,' said Stacey, leaning over the seat of the bus to grab him in an embarrassing cuddle.

So there it was. The silver lining. They'd made up. No problem. Stacey was suitably impressed by his cool and greatly relieved that he hadn't been splattered round Colford's bedroom.

Throughout the rest of the week the only clouds which had loomed were the massive grey ones in the sky, threatening snow and leading to excitable predictions of a white Christmas. Until that morning, when a big, black cloud, with his name on it, descended during English.

School was already winding down, though some teachers insisted they keep working until the bitter end because they were in Year 10 now. Mrs Deale was one.

Not a problem. They were going to carry on with *Macbeth*. Plenty of ghosts, battles and bloody daggers hovering in mid air to keep them entertained. But first Mrs Deale had a few words to say about the homework.

'*Most* of the class,' she emphasized, 'have done it really well, which is one of the reasons it's been so difficult to pick just four to speak in the debate.'

Brad had breathed a sigh of relief at that point. His cunning plan had worked. Almost all were sure to be better than his.

Gavin was chosen as main speaker against the games, which surprised Brad, as Gavin was quite a keen player himself. Brad was even more surprised when the support speaker was announced. It was Stacey.

'I know I said I was on the lookout for new speakers,' Mrs Deale explained to the class, 'but most people used very similar material to support their argument, whereas Stacey has gone for something a bit different, a bit more original.'

Before Brad could wonder what Stacey had managed to come up with, Mrs Deale was onto her next point.

'Choosing speakers in favour of the games,' she said, 'was a bit more difficult. Only four people claimed that the games did not contribute to violent behaviour.'

Four! What had happened to the rest of the class? Loads of them had been against censorship when they were talking last week. Had they been swung by the articles, by their own research or were they simply creeps, writing what they thought Mrs Deale wanted to read?

'As Paula was the only girl to write from that viewpoint,' Mrs Deale said, 'I've chosen her as main speaker.'

Still three to choose from, Brad had thought, smugly. He was safe.

'The other three were all fairly similar,' the teacher had continued. 'Brad's was rather short. Unusual for you, Brad, I thought.'

'Sorry,' Brad had said, hopefully killing off any ideas she might have. 'I just couldn't get that interested in it.'

'That's a shame, Brad,' she'd said, smiling at him, 'because you're going to be the fourth speaker. Though you'll need to add a few more points.'

He'd over-played it! Mrs Deale had realized what he'd been up to! Teachers were a nasty, devious breed and Mrs Deale could be as sharp as any.

Brad's stomach had started churning the minute she'd made her announcement. Mrs Deale had no idea how he felt. Nobody did. They all saw him as outgoing, confident. They didn't know his little weakness. It had never really been an issue. He'd always managed to avoid standing up in public. Ever since that time in Infants when he'd been asked to read in the Christmas Nativity.

He'd been quite sure of himself then. Had been really keen to show off his reading skills, which were way in advance of the rest of the class, who were still struggling to master 'Ben goes to the shop'. Only Brad could read words like 'shepherd' and 'angel'.

He'd insisted on going to school that day, even though he'd been off with a bit of a bug and his mother had said he was still looking decidedly peaky.

In the afternoon, crêpe-paper wings were strapped to backs, donkey masks fastened to snivelling faces and gifts placed in the tiny hands of bickering kings, as doting parents began to flock into the hall.

Brad, the only one dressed in his uniform, took his place at the side, clutching his sheet of paper.

'Are you all right, Brad?' the teacher asked. 'You look very pale. You read beautifully in rehearsal, love. No need to be nervous.'

He wasn't nervous at all. His tummy was making funny noises but it wasn't nerves. He'd felt a bit uncomfortable all day. The bug hadn't quite gone. He just wanted to read, get it over with before he had to rush to the loo again.

They seemed to take ages, walking in from the back, forming their tableau, re-forming it. Pushing one of the shepherds off the raised blocks which were reserved for the angels. Sending Eddie Scott back for his frankincense, which he'd left in the classroom. Persuading little Hannah that she had to hold the Jesus doll, rather than the toy sheep she was trying to wrestle away from Tom. Honestly, Brad had thought, couldn't they get anything right? All they had to do was stand still and look cute. He was the star! Or, at least, he would be if they got on with it.

At last it came. The signal. A slight nod of the teacher's head. Brad stepped forward.

'A long time ago, in a town called Nazareth,' he began, loudly and clearly, 'lived a girl called M—'

He couldn't help it. It came from nowhere. The queasiness, which had happily rumbled round his stomach for the last three days, chose that moment to erupt. Out of his mouth came not the word 'Mary' but a fountain of vomit, projecting onto the feet of the unfortunate spectators in the front row.

Brad was rushed away amidst sympathetic gasps from the audience, as the tableau broke up in a riot of squeals, sniggers and nervous laughter.

He'd ruined it! He'd ruined the Nativity. But that wasn't the worst of it. Nobody would believe it was the bug, he was sure. They'd think he'd got scared. That he was some sort of wimp.

Brad supposed that was where it all stemmed from: the fear of standing up in public, of making a fool of yourself with a hall full of amused eyes, staring. Certainly it had all come flooding back in class today. He wondered if anybody else remembered his particular disgrace. Probably not. Infant school events often descended into chaos and ten years was a long time back.

That's what he tried to tell himself. That he was nearly fifteen now. Not five. He could cope. He wouldn't try to wriggle out of it. It was stupid to be scared. Still, he'd been pleased when the silver lining had presented itself.

'Of course,' Mrs Deale had said, 'we won't have time to

run the debate before Christmas and we won't be able to do it for a week or so after we come back. Can anybody tell me why?'

'Mock exams, miss,' half a dozen people groaned.

'Exactly! Which brings me to the subject of your revision.'

The prospect of mock exams, which had threatened to blight the Christmas holiday, had at that moment seemed positively appealing. With any luck, by the time Mrs Deale had finished getting hysterical about their results, she'd have forgotten all about the video-games debate.

Mocks were one of the reasons Brad had spent so long doing his homework tonight. He wanted to show willing, so his mother wouldn't start moaning about the number of parties he was going to or the time he was spending on his games. Sure enough, his mum popped in a few minutes later, presumably to check that he was working not playing.

'I've just packed up,' Brad said, indicating the couple of bits that were still out, by way of evidence.

His mother nodded and handed him a drink and biscuit. Bad sign, that. He usually had to get his own snacks. This could mean trouble.

'I bumped into Colford earlier,' she said.

It did mean trouble.

'In the shop,' she added, sitting on the end of Brad's bed.

'Oh?' said Brad, a bit perplexed.

He had no idea what might be coming. He hadn't borrowed anything off Colford. Hadn't been mean to him. Far from it. Colford had taken to seeking him out at breaks or lunch times and Brad had let him tag along most days. He was no trouble and could come in quite handy for standing in goal.

'I was asking him what he was doing over Christmas.'

'Getting a whole load of expensive presents, I expect,' said Brad, trying not to sound envious.

'Sitting home on his own, more like,' said Mrs Bradshaw. 'While his dad rolls about town in a drunken stupor.'

'Yeah,' said Brad, thinking of how his own house would swell with deaf grannies, sentimental aunts, over-jolly uncles and irritating cousins. 'Lucky old Col!'

'He didn't seem to have anything planned at all,' said his mother, apparently ignoring him. 'No parties. Nothing.'

'Oh,' said Brad, beginning to get an ominous inkling of what might be coming.

'I mean, why is that? You seem to have dozens lined up.'

'A few,' Brad admitted.

'Well, couldn't you invite Colford?' said his mother, abandoning all attempts at subtlety.

'NO!'

'Why not?'

'They're not my parties, for a start,' Brad mumbled.

'No, but you could make sure he was invited.'

'They're proper parties,' Brad tried. 'Not for kids.'

'He's only a year younger than you! Becky Croft's his age and she goes.'

'How do you know Becky?'

'I don't really, but her mother works at the garage. We often get talking.'

'Yeah well, Becky's different. More sort of grown up. I mean, honestly, can you really see Col at a party? He'd be terrified!'

'Not if you kept an eye on him.'

'NO!' said Brad again. 'Look, I don't mind Col tagging along at school. I don't even mind him coming round here sometimes. I'm nice to him, OK? But I'm not his rotten guardian angel. It's not my fault that his father's a sh—'

'Brad!'

'Or that he hasn't got any friends. Or that he's going to be on his own in a leaky bedroom.'

'And how would you like it, if that was you?' said his mother. 'Honestly, Brad. I don't see why you couldn't invite him to a couple of parties!'

'Because he's a nutter, for a start,' Brad snapped.

'Brad! That's not true and I don't want to hear you saying things like that.'

'Not true?' Brad mumbled. 'How else do you describe someone who talks to statues?'

'Statues?'

'Well, one statue,' said Brad, describing Colford's conversations with Merrick. 'I mean it's bad enough that he talks to it, but then he swears it talks back. Tells him things! I think he sort of likes to pretend that Barnaby Merrick's his dad or something! He even dreams about him. Remember? On the night of the leaky ceiling? I mean, weird or what?'

'A bit creepy, yes,' said Mrs Bradshaw. 'But it doesn't mean he's a nutter, as you so unkindly put it. It means he's lonely. It means he lives in a fantasy world because the real one's so awful. It means there's all the more reason for you to do something to help.'

Brad stared defiantly at his mother. So Col was a bit unhappy. So Col's dad knocked him around. What did Mum expect him to do about it? He wasn't a flaming nanny or a social worker. If she felt so sorry for Colford, why didn't she do something?

'Don't look at me like that!' he snapped.

CHAPTER TEN

They had compromised. Mrs Bradshaw had invited Colford round to the house on Boxing Day and Brad had agreed to take him along to a party on New Year's Eve. It was the easiest to fix. It wasn't at anyone's house, so he didn't have to go through the embarrassment of asking favours.

It was a fancy dress party at Rowanby Village Hall which the girls had decreed they were all going to go along to. So all Brad had to do was discreetly buy another ticket. It was a family do, so there'd be all sorts there from babes in arms to jigging granddads. Everyone would be wearing masks and silly clothes, so Colford wouldn't look too out of place at all.

Boxing Day had been OK. Not an ideal way to spend his birthday but then it never was. His birthday always got swallowed up by festive family gatherings. Colford had come round on a brand new bike, so Brad hadn't bothered asking what he'd got for Christmas. Not until late on in the evening had it come out. The bike was a secondary present! His main gift had been a Game-Scan. Better than all Brad's Christmas and birthday presents put together!

Brad had wanted him to go home and get it straight away but Auntie Ellie had been in the middle of organizing a mind-bogglingly awful game of charades which Mum insisted they join in with. The game had lasted into the early hours, with the adults getting steadily more drunk and the little cousins increasingly fractious.

Colford had stayed overnight and Brad had cycled home with him the following day, with the intention of trying out the Game-Scan. Sadly, Mr Rattersby had been stalking around, looking like he hadn't slept for three days, so Brad had made a quick retreat.

Needless to say, Colford was the only one who'd got a Game-Scan for Christmas. Some of the others had got new games which Brad managed to try out at various parties before Stacey came and tracked him down to spend the rest of the time dancing and kissing, pretending he was enjoying himself. OK, so the kissing stuff was better than the dancing but Stacey always called a halt when it started to get interesting.

'If *that's* all you're interested in,' she would suddenly snap, 'you'd better find Tanya, hadn't you?'

Girls! Who could understand them?

'I thought you cared about *me*,' was another of Stacey's favourites, usually as she was slapping his hand away, 'not what I've got under my jumper!'

'I do,' Brad had said last time. 'Unless you happen to have a Game-Scan tucked away under there.'

Needless to say, she hadn't been amused and had launched into her speech about him preferring his stupid games to her.

'I'm not sure you're ready for a relationship at all, Brad,' she'd accused. 'You're such a kid sometimes. Maybe we should try again when you've grown out of your stupid games.'

Sometimes Brad wasn't sure he was ready for a relation-ship either. Certainly not the serious kind Stacey seemed to have in mind. Sure, she was pretty. Sure, she made him the envy of all his mates. But he couldn't help thinking that he could have more fun round at Colford's with the Blast-Pac and the new Game-Scan. Brad hadn't seen anything of Colford since Boxing Day. He hadn't seen Sunil either – he'd been away since they broke up from school. Tonight, New Year's Eve, would be the only party Sunil was around for. Brad wondered whether Sunil had got a costume sorted out. Stacey, naturally, had organized his for him. The boys' protests that they weren't going to bother dressing up had been smartly brushed aside.

'You have to pay a fine if you don't dress up,' Emma had pointed out, while they were round at her house one afternoon. 'Besides, it'll be fun.'

'You can go as anything you like but we've decided our crowd are all going as pantomime characters,' one of the girls had said, as the boys groaned.

'Can I be Fairy Godmother?' Steve Holton asked.

He was told he was going to be the Dame, wearing one of his gran's old dresses with a couple of strategically placed balloons.

'And we're going as Dick Whittington and his cat,' Stacey had told Brad and she had dragged him off to Emma's bedroom to smother his nose in black stuff and practise drawing on whiskers.

'I look a prat,' he'd quite rightly deduced.

'No you don't,' Stacey told him. 'You look cute.'

She'd folded her arms round him, kissed him and said she loved him. Presumably despite his many faults and obsession with games!

Brad had thought, hoped even, that she was joking. But no, she'd repeated it, whispering into his ear, sending shivers right down to his toes. Confusing him. Love. What did it mean? What did Stacey mean? What was he supposed to say?

Luckily the heavy mood had been broken as Stacey caught sight of herself in the mirror. Black smudges from his nose smeared across her cheeks, causing them both to laugh. Was she disappointed that he hadn't returned the message? Should he have said he loved her? Did he love her? Probably not. She was dead bossy. She irritated him sometimes. But then, on the other hand, she made him feel good. He couldn't imagine not having her around. Simply seeing her made him smile. Touching her . . . well, that produced a different sensation altogether . . . but was it love?

Brad looked at his watch. 15.35. Not even four o'clock, so he had plenty of time. The party didn't start until eight but Stacey had given him strict instructions to be there at quarter to, so she could do his make-up. It was twenty minutes' drive with a bit extra to allow for picking up Sunil and Colford. He'd maybe give Dad a hand with the afternoon milking to earn a bit of extra cash, then there'd still be an hour or so to relax with his games.

★

He was late! Stacey would be furious. And it wasn't his fault. How was he supposed to know Mum was going to insist on him having a shower before he went out. He'd been all ready in his cat-black trousers and polo neck, when she'd made her announcement.

'You smell more like the pantomime cow than a cat,' she'd stated, bluntly. 'Oh, and you'd better wash your hair too!'

Why did he have to wash his hair? He was only going to cover it up with an old, black balaclava which Stacey had kindly sewn some pussy-cat ears onto! It hadn't taken too long, though, so they'd only been five minutes late at Sunil's but he was still busily flapping round trying to put his costume together.

'Honestly,' Sunil's mother had moaned. 'We only got back this morning and he hadn't bothered to tell me it was fancy dress, had he? Only mentioned it an hour ago!'

'I can't find that mask I was going to wear,' Sunil had said, coming down, still in his jeans and sweatshirt.

'Look,' said Brad. 'I'll nip home and grab one of Dad's checked working shirts and Nick's old cowboy hat. Will that do?'

It didn't fit in with the girls' idea of pantomime but what the heck. At least it was something. He had, in fact, grabbed two shirts and hats. He didn't want the same performance at Colford's. And there was absolutely no chance that Col would have got himself organized. While Sunil was getting changed, Brad borrowed some make-up from Sunil's mum to paint on his own nose, eyes and flimsy whiskers. He hoped Stacey would approve.

They drove round to Cross Nook, parking on the road outside Colford's house. No lights were on.

'He's gone out,' said Brad, anxiously checking his watch. 'Come on. Let's go.'

'He's probably fallen asleep,' said his dad, beeping the horn, setting the dogs off barking. 'That should wake him up!'

After a few seconds' waiting, Brad got out of the car. It was clear his dad wasn't going to drive on until they'd checked properly. The front door didn't have a bell or a knocker, so Brad banged on the wood. No answer. He was just about to turn and walk away when his dad joined him.

'Bit worrying,' he said, frowning. 'Colford knew you were picking him up, right?'

'Yeah but he probably forgot.'

'I don't know,' said his dad. 'I don't like it. I think we ought to check round the back.'

'Geroff!' said Brad. 'The dogs are round there.'

'They're usually locked up,' said his dad, leading the way up the side path.

There was quite a bit of land round the back. A garden, full of junk. The wire compound where the dogs were kept. A large shed and beyond that a small orchard, gone wild. They could see it all fairly clearly, as the kitchen light was on and everything was coated with a fine, white dusting of snow.

Mr Bradshaw checked the back door and disappeared

inside, calling Colford's name. Brad stood by the open door, glanced inside and decided against following his dad.

As he turned back, the dogs fell silent and he saw the ghost. It was standing by the now slightly open door of the shed. The faint pinkish light from inside the shed cast an eerie glow onto the uniformed figure. A soldier. A soldier with a blood-soaked bandage around his head. Brad felt his legs go weak as the apparition moved.

'Is this OK?' said the ghost.

'Col?' said Brad, coming to his senses.

'Is this all right, for a costume?' Colford repeated, as Mr Bradshaw came out to join them and Sunil's head appeared over the side gate.

'Cor!' said Sunil. 'Makes my cowboy outfit look a bit sick. That looks dead authentic.'

It certainly did. Brad had recognized the uniform immediately. First World War. They'd studied it last year in history. And the school always made a big deal out of Remembrance Day, with the Merrick connection and everything.

Somehow, though, Brad hadn't thought Colford was the type to go to the trouble of hiring an elaborate costume, which is why 'the ghost' had given him a bit of a fright.

'So it's OK?' Colford repeated. 'I wasn't sure. I'm not very good at fancy dress.'

'It's more than OK,' said Sunil. 'It's brill! Where did you get it from?'

86

Colford turned slightly, indicating with his head towards the shed.

'My dad collects war stuff,' he said. 'Buys and sells it on the Net.'

'You mean to say that's real!' Brad squeaked. 'An original! A genuine uniform.'

Colford nodded, as though it was nothing special, opened the shed door fully and led the way inside.

'I made the bandage myself,' Colford said, proudly. 'The blood's ketchup. Good, isn't it?'

Nobody answered. They were too busy staring. Long, rough tables, piled high with stuff, were laid out in the shed. A cross between a jumble sale and a miniature war museum, Brad thought. Wars through the ages and across the nations. There were photographs, postcards, medals, uniforms and weapons. Lots of weapons. Old guns. Evil-looking machetes. Knives. A whole boxful of knives.

He wondered for a moment what Sunil would make of the Nazi flags plastered across the walls. The swastikas. The racist propaganda. What anybody would make of it! Was this what Colford's dad actually did for a living? Was this how he made his money? Trading in war memorabilia?

Not that there was necessarily anything wrong with it. No more than trading in rare stamps or antique furniture. There was nothing to suggest that this was actually illegal. Though, knowing Colford's dad, you couldn't help but wonder.

'Don't tell my dad I let you see this,' Colford was

urging Mr Bradshaw. 'I'm not supposed to let anyone see. Dad doesn't want anyone coming round, nicking stuff.'

'Oh, er, yes,' said Mr Bradshaw, thoughtfully. 'And does your dad know you've borrowed the uniform?'

'He's away,' said Colford.

'Look, I'm sorry,' said Mr Bradshaw, 'but I really don't think you can wear that for the fancy dress.'

'But you said it looked OK.'

'It does! It looks too good, that's the trouble. What if it gets damaged, gets something spilt on it? What would your dad have to say to that? And what if anyone asks where it came from?'

'We'll say it's a replica,' Brad said, becoming anxious about all the time they were wasting. 'We'll say he hired it from that place on the other side of town. And it won't get damaged. It's not that sort of party!'

'I don't know,' his dad mused.

'Oh, come on,' said Brad. 'Col looks great. He's bound to win first prize. He'll be dead pleased,' he added in a whisper. 'It's not often Col gets the chance to shine a bit, is it?'

'All right,' his dad finally agreed. 'But you just be careful, Colford. I don't fancy answering to your dad, if it gets ruined!'

'It won't,' said Colford, wandering over to the far corner of the shed, next to a cabinet full of guns. He picked something up from the side of the cabinet.

'You don't think you're taking that!' Mr Bradshaw said, staring at the rifle.

'It's not loaded or anything,' said Colford. 'It's not even real. This one's a replica.'

'No!' said Mr Bradshaw, firmly. 'Definitely not.'

They left without the rifle. Colford used about twelve different locks to secure the shed door, checking and re-checking every one, before letting one of the dogs loose in the cottage to guard it and going through the multiple lock procedure once again. Mr Rattersby sure was paranoid about his possessions. Cross Nook had a non-existent crime rate, unless you counted Mr Rattersby's own dubious activities.

As cat, cowboy and soldier piled into the car, Brad checked his watch. 21.09. He was going to be ages late. Where had all the time gone? Stacey would be furious.

Why hadn't she phoned him? Why hadn't she answered the dozen or so messages he'd left?

His dad turned the ignition on the old Land-Rover. It coughed, spluttered and coughed again.

'It'll be all right in a minute,' he assured them. 'It's the cold weather. Old girl can't cope any more.'

After fifteen minutes, they gave up and phoned Sunil's mother to come to the rescue. Neither Brad's parents nor Sunil's were going to the party, Brad's because they weren't really late-night people and Sunil's because the twins had both come back from their little holiday with nasty colds.

So Sunil's mum eventually dropped them off outside Rowanby Village Hall, telling them she'd be back around one o'clock to pick them up.

'Hardly worth bothering,' muttered Sunil. 'It's gone ten already!'

'Don't be such a misery,' his mother said. 'Enjoy yourselves. You look great in that uniform, Colford!'

'Thanks,' said Colford, beaming. 'I'm going to pretend I'm Charles Merrick. He fought in the First World War, you know. Mr Merrick told...'

Brad grabbed Colford's arm and dragged him off before he could confess that he'd got his information from a talking statue!

CHAPTER ELEVEN

1915

'What do you think, Father?'

Barnaby Merrick turned away from his son. He couldn't bear to see that uniform.

'You know what I think, Charles,' he said, walking towards the window of their London home. 'I think it's madness.'

The minute the war had begun, Charles had wanted to join up. Barnaby had dissuaded him.

'But why, Charles? There's no need. The whole sorry business will be over by Christmas. You'll see.'

But it wasn't over. Far from it.

'What do you expect me to do?' Charles had said after the first Zeppelin raids in January. 'Nothing? Stand by until it's too late? Hide myself away with all the other cowards.'

'You're not a coward, Charles.'

'No, I'm not. You brought me up to be tough, didn't you? You always wanted me to be strong. Brave. Honourable. And for what? This isn't like you, Father. I simply don't understand you any more.'

But was it so difficult to understand? God, your country, they were important. Worth standing up for. Worth fighting for. And, if he was young enough, fit enough to go himself, he would. But Charles. That was a different matter. How could he be expected to sacrifice Charles?

Burton's lads had joined up. Every last one of them. That was

91

what had made the difference. When Tom had been killed. When they had read, with Burton, the letter commending Tom's bravery.

'You can't stop me, sir,' Charles had said. 'And, even if you could, how long will it be before I have to go? There's already talk of conscription.'

'It won't come to that! The Germans won't hold out. There'll be no conscription.'

'There will. And I'm not going to wait to be rounded up, dragged in kicking and screaming. It's my duty to volunteer. Surely you can see that?'

Duty. Honour. King and Country. Words, words. What did they mean? And did they have anything to do with Charles's eagerness to volunteer? Or, Barnaby reflected, was he simply caught up in all the rhetoric, the talk of glory? The chance to live out his childhood fantasies, played on the lawn at Merrick Hall with young Sam Burton. When the good always won. When the dead always got up and walked away.

Charles had barely turned twenty. No more than a boy. What did he know? What did he understand?

'I know how to handle a gun,' Charles had assured him. 'I can take care of myself.'

No doubt Tom Burton had thought the same. None of them went into it believing they were going to die. But they had. Thousands of them. Already.

'Please, Father,' Charles was saying. 'I have to go now.'

Barnaby turned and shook his son's outstretched hand, before pulling him towards him in a momentary embrace. Charles moved away a little too quickly, clearly embarrassed by such displays of emotion, now that he was a grown man.

'You won't come to the station, then?'

Barnaby shook his head, walking with Charles only as far as the door before returning to the window. From there he watched as his son left the house, striding, almost bouncing, down the street. Willing him to turn back and wave. But he didn't. Too eager to be gone.

Wearily, Barnaby turned away and walked slowly over to the sofa. His hip was troubling him again. It had never been right since he'd taken a fall from his horse, two years ago. He was only forty-nine but felt older. Especially now. Especially now he was alone.

'Oh, Anne,' he said, staring at the portrait on the opposite wall. 'You would have been so proud of him.'

Pride, anger, frustration, fear, love. A dangerous cocktail of emotions, threatening to destroy him. All he could do was wait and hope, believe what the doctor had once told him, that Charles was a natural fighter, a survivor. Hang onto the last words Charles had said to him at the door before he left.

'Don't worry, Father. I won't let you down. I'll be back. I promise.'

CHAPTER TWELVE

Brad leant against the wall of Rowanby Village Hall. His black-cat balaclava, complete with silly ears, was no protection against the driving snow which hit his face, blending with the make-up, running grey gunge into his eyes, making them sting. A sad black cat out in the cold.

It wasn't fair. It just wasn't fair.

'Brad. Are you coming in? They're about to do "Auld Lang Syne",' said the soldier who'd just arrived at his side.

Colford visibly flinched as Brad swore at him.

'Brad, what's wrong?'

'Nothing,' said Brad, before repeating his original message.

Colford's bandage had come loose and was hanging over his face. He gave a quick tug. Pulled it off. Looked at it.

'I came first, you know,' he said. 'In the Fancy Dress. I won.'

'Big deal, Colford. Now for the third time...'

Even Colford wasn't thick skinned enough to ignore a third message. He scurried off inside, head down, dejected. Brad barely noticed. He had enough of his own problems. Or rather one big problem. Stacey.

Granted, it had been very late by the time they'd arrived. He'd looked round for Stacey straight away but hadn't found her. He'd bought himself a drink, sat down with Sunil and some other lads, watching the dance floor, seeing if he could pick out Stacey's Dick Whittington hat with the huge, green feather. But it had been mostly oldies dancing, with some little kids running around.

He'd tried the kitchens. The small games room. He'd tried phoning her, in case she'd gone home in a huff. No answer. He'd even asked Emma to check the ladies' loo.

'Where the heck is she then?' he'd asked.

'Don't ask me,' Emma had shrugged. 'Haven't seen her since about quarter to ten. She was pretty mad by then.'

'Just because I was late?'

'No, Brad. Because you're always late. Or missing. Or mucking her about.'

It wasn't true. But there'd been no point arguing. It was clear whose side Emma was on. It became even clearer a while later, when Emma came mincing up to him.

'Have you tried upstairs?'

He had, earlier on. But there was nothing up there. Just a storage area where 'Mums and Toddlers' kept their toys and where surplus chairs were stacked. Goaded by the snide hint in Emma's voice, he'd gone up again. Halfway up. He'd stopped when he saw the discarded hat with the green feather on the half landing, where the stairs turned. He'd looked up to see Stacey kissing a gorilla. Or rather Philandering Phil in a gorilla suit, minus the head, which was lying alongside Stacey's hat.

Brad rather wished it was Phil's real head he was kicking, as he booted the furry face towards them. Not a bad shot, considering it had to cover the last five steps, before it made contact with Stacey's back. She'd turned round, her face slightly flushed, her blue eyes brighter than ever.

'Hi,' she'd said, before turning back to devour Phil.

Brad bent down, squashed some snow into a ball and hurled it at the fence. Then another and another. So that was love, was it? The sort of love that disintegrated like a snowball, just because someone was a couple of hours late. Or maybe it was nothing to do with the lateness at all. Maybe it wouldn't have mattered what time he'd turned up. She'd probably arranged to meet Phil, anyway. It had probably been going on for weeks, behind his back. No doubt everyone had been having a good laugh at him, on the quiet! She'd made him look a right idiot.

He gave up throwing and turned to kicking as the first strains of 'Auld Lang Syne' came blasting out in a confusion of raucous voices. For some reason Brad found himself singing different words. Maybe it was Colford's uniform which had brought it to his mind. The song which soldiers in the trenches used to sing to the tune of 'Auld Lang Syne'. Not exactly difficult to remember. The words were a bit repetitive, to say the least.

'We're here because, we're here because . . .

We're here because we're here.

We're here because, we're here because . . .

We're here because, we're here.'

Here, outside in the snow, with everyone else in there, shrieking and shouting 'Happy New Year'. And slimy Phil sticking his tongue down Stacey's throat.

'Happy New Year!'

The last of the shouts, followed by enough bangs, pops

96

and cracks to make you think the First World War had started all over again.

'Happy New Year,' he muttered to himself. He waited until the sounds of excessive revelry had died down and slunk back inside. The slow music had started. The elderly and the very young had begun to drift home, leaving the dance floor to the teens and young adults. The couples. He sat down at an empty table near the back, trying not to stare at Stacey and Phil. Not that they'd have noticed. How could she do this to him?

He looked around for Sunil, desperately needing someone to talk to. He was on the dance floor. Sunil never danced! He was with a girl! It took Brad a moment to recognize her in the flashing lights and tangle of limbs. It was Gail. A Year 11 girl. Sunil had chosen a great time to become someone's toy boy.

Even Colford was dancing. OK, so it was only with matronly Miss Wattle, their old junior school teacher, who was chatting away to him, telling him how great he looked in that uniform, making him blush and break out into a smile which threatened to split his face.

Everybody was smiling. Everybody was laughing. Except him.

Brad pulled off the balaclava and rubbed it across his face to get rid of the fading whiskers and black smudges. He looked at the clock, desperate for Sunil's mother to turn up. He just wanted to go home, go to bed and never get up again.

★

The first week back at school after the holiday was utter misery. Sunil droning on about Gail and how she'd fancied him from afar for ages. How she'd said he was nicer than all the Year 11 lads put together.

'Yeah, well, I wouldn't believe what girls say,' Brad had growled.

'I'm sorry about you and Stacey,' Sunil had tried.

'Don't be. I don't care. It doesn't matter. I was getting fed up, anyway. Who needs girls to organize your life and boss you around? I can do what I want now.'

Stacey had sort of apologized. Claimed she hadn't meant it to happen like that. But she wasn't trying to make up. She was clearly besotted with Phil. How could she be so stupid? Didn't she know what he was like?

Not that Brad cared about Stacey, he told himself. But the break-up had changed other things too. He'd reluctantly agreed to Stacey's suggestion that they could still be friends. But that didn't mean he wanted to sit next to her in class. And, as she settled in the usual place with Emma, Sunil and the rest of their group, it had been Brad who'd had to sit elsewhere.

The next two weeks were even worse. Trying to concentrate on mock exams, sitting up half the night trying to catch up on the revision he should have done earlier. Getting increasingly tired, stressed and irritable. Taking it out on 'poor' Nick. Landing himself in bother at home.

It wasn't until the end of January that Brad felt he could really relax. The trouble was, there was nothing to do. The weather was foul. Sunil was still seeing Gail. And when he wasn't, he was hanging out with the old crowd. Stacey's crowd. And Brad was still trying to avoid Stacey.

He'd bought a couple of new games with his Christmas money, games his mother wouldn't approve of. But even playing wasn't so much fun on your own. With nobody to boast to when you'd cracked a level or developed a particularly neat strategy.

In desperation, at the weekend he'd phoned Colford. Even Colford had seemed quieter, more remote than ever. Not that keen to come over.

'You can come here, if you like,' Colford had said. 'It's all right. Dad's out.'

Brad was surprised to find Colford wearing the First World War uniform, looking exactly as he'd done on the night of the fancy dress, only with a hat instead of the blood-soaked bandage.

'What you doing, Col?' Brad had asked.

'Sharpening this,' Colford had answered, as if sitting around in a First World War uniform sharpening a piece of wood with a rather evil-looking knife was perfectly reasonable behaviour.

'I meant why are you wearing that again?'

'It looks good,' said Colford. 'Everyone said it looked good. I won. Everyone said it looked good.'

'And what does your dad say?' Brad asked, loading 'Survival' into the machine.

'He doesn't like me touching his stuff,' Colford muttered. 'Want to play?'

'No. You play.'

So Brad had played alone.

'What are you making then, Col?' he'd asked, between games.

'Nothing.'

Nothing seemed about right. The pile of shavings on the floor was growing, as the piece of wood got smaller, developing no recognizable shape. Fairly typical, meaningless Colford behaviour, so Brad went back to his game.

'There wasn't any bother from your dad about wearing that uniform for the party, was there?' Brad asked a while later, when Colford had gone on to slicing up an old bicycle tyre into neat little pieces.

'Wasn't there?'

'I mean, does he know? Did he have a go at you?'

'No. He hasn't seen me wearing it. He doesn't know.'

Brad's next attempt at conversation came just before he was about to leave.

'Hey, Col. You never showed me your Game-Scan. What's it like?'

'It's like a plastic box with a lid that lifts up to put your pictures in and—'

'No. I meant, what's it like in action? Does it make a difference to the games? Can you use it with any of them?'

'I don't know,' said Colford. 'It doesn't work.'

He walked over to a cupboard and presented Brad with a box.

'Dad's had a go and I've had a go but it doesn't work. Dad said he'll have another look, when he's got time.'

'But it's brand new,' said Brad. 'It should work. Tell you what, I've got to go now but I'll pop back tomorrow and try and set it up, eh?'

'No,' said Colford. 'Take it with you. It's useless. It doesn't work.'

'I can't,' said Brad. 'Remember?'

Colford clearly didn't. Brad thought about it for a moment. He'd promised never to borrow any of Colford's stuff. But what harm could it do? Just overnight. Just till he got it set up and working. Then he'd bring it back. It'd cheer Colford up a bit and he certainly looked as though he needed cheering up. Like a real soldier who'd just been ordered over the top.

Brad took the box.

'Col,' he said, 'is there anything wrong?'

'Yes. It doesn't work.'

'No. With you, I mean. You look right fed up.'

'I'm OK.'

'You'd say, wouldn't you,' he tried, 'if anybody was bugging you at school or anything? I mean, I know I've been a bit out of it for a while, with mocks and Stacey and stuff.'

'It's OK,' said Col. 'I talk to Mr Merrick. He listens to me.'

'Yeah,' said Brad. 'I know. But it's sort of difficult for Barnaby Merrick to *do* anything, isn't it? Him being sort of dead and a statue and all that. So, if you needed something sorted, you'd let me know, eh?'

'Sure, Brad.'

It was hard to tell with Colford, Brad thought, as he cycled home in the rain. He was never what you'd call a great communicator. Goodness knows what Barnaby Merrick made of Col's ramblings! The poor man was probably writhing in his grave, screaming to get away. But if it helped Col to talk to a slab of marble, what the heck! It was better than brooding.

It didn't do to brood, according to Brad's mother. To keep things bottled up.

Brad half smiled to himself. Who was he to talk? Wasn't that what he'd done about Stacey? Kept it bottled up? But who could he tell? Who would understand how he felt? He barely understood it himself.

One minute he was daydreaming about them getting back together, living happily ever after. The next he was creating wild fantasies which usually involved something decidedly unpleasant happening to Stacey and always, always, involved Philandering Phil dying a slow and gruesome death.

CHAPTER THIRTEEN

Phil was avoiding him. He might be in the Upper Sixth. He might drive a posh, red sports car. He might have dated every good-looking girl in the school, but he was still a wimp.

Brad couldn't imagine what girls saw in Phil. Apart from the car, of course. He was quite small, looked younger than most of the Year 11s and wore wire-framed specs. Emma said he had charisma, whatever that was supposed to be. But she should know. She'd been one of his victims, briefly, at the start of the year. She reckoned he was mature, romantic, made girls feel special. But Brad couldn't see what was mature about drifting from girl to girl or how they could feel so special when Phil dumped them after the first couple of dates.

Stacey had already lasted longer than most with Phil. More's the pity. Over a month now. So maybe he'd changed. Or maybe, thought Brad, bitterly, he just liked stealing other people's girlfriends. Watching them suffer.

Well, he wasn't going to get away with it. Brad couldn't wait to see Phil's face when he realized he was waiting for him. The shock. The panic. When he saw the gun.

It was a disappointment, of course. Partly because Phil's expression never changed. The self-satisfied smirk didn't even flicker, even when Brad fired. How could it? The Game-Scan wasn't that good.

Brad had got it working easily enough. He'd scanned in a picture of himself at first, playing the hero ghost-buster in 'Haunted'. Then, once the novelty of that had worn off, he'd had his idea. He'd 'borrowed' a photo of Phil from the music notice-board at school. Phil gloating when he'd won yet another award for playing his saxophone. He'd scanned it into one of the gorier games he'd bought with his Christmas money. Thought he'd have a bit of fun, blasting the smile from Phil's face.

Only, in the event, it wasn't that much fun. Brad now felt faintly sick, as he reached over and shut down the machine. Incredibly sick, in fact. Maybe Stacey was right. Maybe there was something sinister and unnatural about shooting someone you knew. Even a virtual someone. Even someone in a game.

Not a brilliant time to be having reservations. Not with the debate coming up the next day, when he was supposed to argue, convincingly, that the games and all the associated gadgets were perfectly harmless.

It was raining, which was bad news. The hall was packed. People drifting in, deciding there was nothing better to do than watch Lawrence Bradshaw make an idiot of himself. The four of them were already up on the stage. Gavin, Stacey and Paula, looking cool and in control; Brad knowing he was turning paler by the minute, clutching his notes tightly, with both hands, to stop himself biting his nails. He'd worked on his speech. He knew it was good. But could he deliver it? Or should he just bolt now, while he still had time?

Too late. Mrs Deale was already introducing them. Announcing the debate.

'This House believes that violent video games lead to violent behaviour and should be banned.'

Brad tried to force himself to listen, as Gavin stood up to speak in favour of the motion. It wasn't easy to concentrate with his head already spinning and sweat breaking out on his forehead. But he had to pay attention. Try to pick up on any clever little points Gavin might make.

Gavin spoke clearly and well but it was fairly standard stuff. Quoting statistics from dodgy surveys, giving examples of children who'd killed, who might have been influenced by the games.

'The point about shoot-'em-up games,' Gavin was saying, 'is that they train children as young as seven to be terrifyingly accurate marksmen. How else could you explain the case in America where a boy went into a playground, fired fifteen shots in rapid succession and hit fifteen moving targets? Thirteen primary school children died that day. Another two were severely wounded.'

Admittedly nasty, Brad thought. And Gavin was deliberately playing on emotions, milking it for all it was worth. But was he proving anything? Brad wasn't sure. The jellified mass, which had once been a perfectly good brain, refused to function. He hoped Paula was managing to think a bit more clearly.

She obviously was. Almost before poor Gavin had

finished, she leapt to her feet to reply. Her style was quite different. Whereas Gavin had been serious and intense, Paula was mocking, almost jokey. Brad vaguely wondered whether it was the right approach.

'I have a confession to make,' Paula began. 'Last night I played "Target". So watch out, anyone who's thinking of voting against me, because, according to Gavin, I've probably become a crack-shot psychotic with an automatic pistol tucked up my knickers...But what Gavin didn't tell you, of course,' she continued, 'was about the background that American boy came from. He lived in an isolated shack with a drug-addicted mother and a grandfather whose hobby was shooting the local wildlife. Dad was already in prison for armed robbery. So isn't it possible that the boy learnt his marksmanship, not from the video games but from shooting hapless raccoons with his grandfather?'

Good old Paula, Brad thought, trying to stay focused, trying to take it all in. She'd certainly done her research. Both she and Gavin made long speeches. Brad followed the twists and turns of Paula's arguments, noting with satisfaction the hush which had descended on the hall. The rapt attention.

'Children through the ages,' Paula was concluding, 'have played violent games, with sticks, little plastic guns or on screens. It's human nature. It's part of growing up. Learning to distinguish the real from the unreal. Our parents played them. Our grandparents played them. They've had their fun. So maybe they should stop preaching and leave us alone to have ours?'

Stacey had to wait a while until the applause died down, before she could stand up and have her say. Brad wondered what line she was going to take. Mrs Deale had hinted that Stacey had been a bit original in her argument. Done something different.

It didn't seem that different at first. Stacey was obviously thinking on her feet and adapting her speech as she went along, as she began exactly where Paula left off.

'Paula was quite right,' Stacey said, immediately grabbing people's attention. 'Children have always played violent games. I expect the little Neanderthals in their caves played them. Perhaps Viking junior had his own tiny horned helmet and pretend sword. Frontier kids in the West no doubt fired toy guns at imaginary Native Americans, in preparation for slaughtering real ones. Because, make no mistake, that's what it is. Pretend violence is a preparation for the real thing.'

Rubbish, Brad thought. Games are games. Nothing more, nothing less. Still, Stacey had a horrible habit of sounding right, whatever drivel she was spouting.

'And isn't it wonderful,' she continued, 'to know that in all these millions of years of evolution, we haven't changed? We still indulge our darker basic instincts.'

Brad thought, miserably, about the basic instincts she might have been indulging with Philandering Phil, who was sitting, transfixed, right in the front row.

'Only now,' Stacey said, 'we can do it so much more easily, can't we? We don't even have to trouble our imaginations. All the sick, psychotic images we could possibly want are all laid out for us on a screen.'

Great, Brad reflected. This was all standard and expected stuff which his own speech would easily counter balance, if his legs would stop shaking enough to allow him to stand up. Where was the stunning originality Mrs Deale had promised?

'But sadly, we can perpetrate real violence more easily too,' Stacey was saying. 'The technology which gives us our games also gives us weapons of mass destruction. And, like the games, they're rather remote, impersonal, aren't they?'

Fine. But what had all that got to do with anything? thought Brad, as his own turn to speak loomed ever nearer.

'What worries me,' said Stacey, earnestly, 'is not just the odd lunatic. The occasional, unbalanced nutter who might, under the immediate influence of the games, go out and shoot someone for real. But the more general, underlying acceptance of extreme violence which these games are forcing on a whole generation of kids. Kids who might grow up to be the leaders, the politicians, of the future.'

Now this, Brad thought, might be a bit original but it was definitely far fetched. He scribbled down a few notes to add to his prepared speech.

'Amidst all the horrors which still go on in the world,' Stacey said, 'I think there has been some cause for optimism. An increasing desire for peaceful solutions. But are we now putting this at risk? How safe will we feel in a world where the people with their hands on the nuclear trigger, or on the stock piles of chemical weapons, have been brought up on a diet of shoot-'em-up games?'

Talk about over-reaction! Typical Stacey, that was. Video games lead to outbreak of World War Three! Neat ending, though, Brad admitted, trying to make his body move from his seat. But, no. Stacey hadn't quite finished.

'I want to end,' she said, 'by reminding you of some words from our benefactor, Barnaby Merrick. A man, remember, who saw, not one, but two World Wars. A man who knew all about the dark side of human nature.'

Well maybe he did, thought Brad, but he certainly wouldn't have known anything about techno-games.

'Scribbled on the margin of one of Merrick's diaries,' Stacey informed them, 'dated 1917, are the words: "What game are they playing, these generals? Ignoring the reality of death, chasing childish fantasies. Dangerous illusions of glory. The very work of the devil."

'Ask yourselves ... What kind of devil's work are the fantasies in these sick, psychotic modern games capable of releasing?' Stacey said, her voice rising to a crescendo. 'And do pupils sitting here, in Barnaby Merrick's former home, really want to vote in favour of them?'

Stacey flicked her hair back as she finished, turning and smiling at Brad. That just about finished him off. He'd been all prepared to get a grip, bluff it out and now Stacey had reduced him to jelly by the simple movement of a few lip muscles.

He stood up, making the mistake of glancing out at the hall, seeing all those eyes staring back at him. Phil's eyes,

Colford's eyes, Mrs Deale's eyes. He might have been all right, if he'd stuck exactly to his prepared speech. But he didn't. He tried to do what Paula and Stacey had done. To add a few references to the previous speaker. It was coming out all wrong, he knew. Hesitant, not loud enough. A muttering, stuttering, mumbling, jumbling tumble of disjointed words.

He had something to say about Stacey's far-fetched war connection, but couldn't quite make it sound sensible. He had a good point about Merrick too but couldn't remember what it was. So he stumbled on, cursing himself as his papers visibly shook in his hands. He felt a complete prat.

He didn't even finish off properly or dramatically, as the others had done. He could feel himself hurrying the ending, slumping back in his seat, relieved it was all over. Applause was merely polite. He knew he hadn't exactly shone. But, on the other hand, at least he hadn't thrown up. Still shaking slightly, Brad listened to Mrs Deale thanking the speakers and reminding the audience what they were supposed to be voting on.

'This House believes that violent video games lead to violent behaviour and should be banned.'

Brad quickly assessed the situation. There were more girls in the hall than boys, so that probably wasn't in his favour. Paula's speech had got most applause, but then, his had got least. Stacey was dead popular and had loads of friends, which shouldn't influence the situation but probably would.

So his guess was that he and Paula would only get about a quarter of the votes. But when the hands went up, it wasn't even that good. Nowhere near. A veritable forest of hands waving in support of the motion, of banning the games.

'Er...anyone against?' said Mrs Deale.

Only six hands went up and two of those belonged to Colford, so five votes in all. Five measly votes!

Stacey flashed Brad another smile, an irritating mixture of triumph and sympathy. As they left the stage, Philandering Phil was there, putting his arm round Stacey whilst winking at Kara, the Deputy Head Girl, behind Stacey's back.

Stacey had once said Phil never played techno-games. No wonder! How could he possibly find the time?

'You were really good, Brad,' said Colford, sidling up to him.

'So who cares what *you* think?' snarled Brad, pushing past him.

Out in the fresh air, he regretted it. How low and petty could you get? Snapping at Colford just because you'd lost a debate. Just because Stacey and Phil were gloating.

'You OK, Brad?' said Colford's voice at his shoulder.

'Yeah...I'm OK, thanks.'

'I'm just gonna tell Mr Merrick that Stacey mentioned him in the debate,' said Colford, ambling towards the statue. 'I think he'll like that, won't he?'

'Yeah,' said Brad. 'I expect so. Everyone else did.'

'I like to tell him things to cheer him up, sometimes,'

said Colford. 'He had such a sad life. I'd like to be able to make him smile.'

'You've made me smile,' said Brad, laughing in spite of everything. 'Will that do?'

CHAPTER FOURTEEN

1916

Three letters lay spread out on Barnaby Merrick's desk at
Merrick Hall. The first was dated October 1915.

Dear Father,

I am writing this from the field hospital, but there is no need
to worry. My wound is a mere scratch, thanks to the bravery of
Sam Burton. About a dozen of us were holding a crater, in front
of our trenches, when we came under heavy bombardment and
had to withdraw. I was knocked off my feet by a tremendous
blast and fell to the ground as a torrent of mud rained down, half
burying me.

The foul stuff was in my throat, nostrils and mouth. I
thought I was done for. But Sam came back, digging me free
with his bare hands, braving the continual burst of fire, dragging
me to safety. Not content with that, he went back a second time
for Private Jones.

He had trouble getting Jones out. Jones clung onto him,
refusing to budge, breaking two of Sam's fingers in the struggle.
Sam, in agony himself and still under heavy fire, ended up
carrying Jones.

We all thought Jones had taken a shot to the legs, but
mercifully no. The paralysis was temporary, brought on by
shock. Physically he's fine now but he hasn't been passed fit to
go back yet. He screams at the slightest noise and pushes away

all food, insisting it's crawling with maggots. He just sits day after day, staring at a picture of his wife and kids, mumbling to himself.

Poor man's not very popular on the ward, I'm afraid. Even the doctor lost patience yesterday, and accused him of malingering. I think Jones would rally, given time. He's no coward. But I fear he'll be sent back to the trenches before he's ready. Like Sam said, when he went back with his broken fingers still bandaged up, we need every man we can get and who cares whether they've got the odd bit missing!

Tell Burton there's talk of a V.C. for Sam. He'll be so proud. As for me, I have to say I'm glad of the chance to rest and the food here is slightly better than in the trenches (maggot free, despite what Jones says!). I'll be fighting fit and back in action soon. Some are not so fortunate. The lad in the next bed has lost an arm and is due to be sent home tomorrow. Poor blighter. He insists he'll be back to help in some capacity. Such is the bravery of most of the men here!

I trust you are well and beg you not to worry about recent setbacks which you may have read about. Victory is in sight, I am sure. And, despite everything, spirits remain remarkably high. I am struck by the capacity of the British Tommy to laugh and joke in the face of all manner of adversity and I'm proud to serve as one them.

Your loving son,
Charles

Barnaby's face creased as he read it again. Too much talk of bravery and pride. Burton had understood. Had wished that

114

Sam wasn't quite so brave. That he didn't take such risks. Burton had lost three sons already.

'I don't want their bloody medals,' he'd cried out. 'I want my boys.'

The second letter from Charles was shorter, dated August 1916.

Dear Father,

How can I write of the pit of hell into which we've descended? The grey faces, more ghosts than men. The mangled limbs claimed as much by barbed wire as by bombs. The interminable noise which drives men to madness. Poor Private Jones, never the same since that business in the crater, facing a firing squad for desertion.

Night after night I see him, haunting my dreams.

I wake to the sound of screams. Not always my own. Our dreams, I fear, make cowards of us all.

Remember us in your prayers.

Yours ever,

Charles

The third, shorter still, dated just three weeks ago, Barnaby couldn't bear to look at.

A brief, standard notification that Charles Barnaby Merrick had died bravely at the Somme.

CHAPTER FIFTEEN

'What's going on with Col, Brad?' said Sunil, as they walked home together on the Friday after the disastrous debate.

'I don't know? What do you mean?'

'You haven't heard?' said Sunil, incredulously.

Brad shook his head. He'd been vaguely aware that Colford hadn't been on the school bus on Monday. He'd meant to look out for him on Tuesday but by the time they reached Cross Nook, Brad's attention had been totally focused on Stacey. She had cried the whole journey, not caring who was watching or listening.

The inevitable had happened. Phil had dumped her for Kara, the Deputy Head Girl. A glutton for punishment, that one. She'd been out with Phil before. Twice. Stacey had sought Brad out, day after day. But any fond hopes he might have entertained about them getting back together had been quickly squashed. He was no more than a shoulder to cry on. An incredibly soggy shoulder by the end of the week.

Stacey was a mess. Totally in pieces. So genuinely screwed up, he couldn't even gloat. All he could do was listen and touch the photo of Phil which was in his jacket pocket. He'd been meaning to put the photograph back on the notice-board. But no. He'd keep it a while longer. He'd have no trouble blasting Phil's nasty, smug face now, he was sure.

'You haven't heard about that business in the gym?'
Sunil was repeating.

'No. What happened?'

'Col apparently turned up for games yesterday, without his kit so Mr Pearse chucked some stuff out of the "lost" box at him and told him to get changed. Col refused.'

'Refused Mr Pearse?' said Brad. 'Col wouldn't have the guts to do that . . . unless . . .'

'Right,' said Sunil.

'How bad?' said Brad.

'Pretty nasty. Gail's brother's in Col's class. He said Mr Pearse insisted, till Col took his shirt off. Then he made him put it right back on again and dragged him off to the medical room.'

'Why though?' said Brad. 'I thought things were more settled. Why's his dad started hitting him again?'

'I dunno,' said Sunil. 'I thought you might know something. Col talks to you.'

'He hasn't,' said Brad, immediately feeling guilty, knowing he hadn't given Colford much chance recently. 'But I had a feeling something might be wrong when I went round the other week. He was all sort of agitated, in his own quiet little way. Sitting there chopping up bits of wood and bike tyre. Wearing that First World War uniform.'

'Sounds a bit loopy even for Col,' said Sunil. 'Did you tell anyone?'

'I mentioned it to Mum,' said Brad. 'But you know what Col's like. Mum reckons he lives in a fantasy world 'cos the real one's so awful. But you can't do anything. People have tried before.'

'Gail's brother said they took Col up to the hospital and called in the social worker but they obviously haven't done much, have they? 'Cos he was back on the bus again today, so he must still be at home, mustn't he? Gail said it's not right and they should take him into care or something. But they've tried that, haven't they?'

'Three or four times, that I remember,' said Brad. 'Thing is, Col won't ever admit it's his dad who's done it. He makes up stories about falling off walls or walking into things. Like Mum says — a complete fantasy world. They always have to drag him away from that cottage, kicking and screaming. Whatever happens, whatever his dad does, Col doesn't want to leave him.'

'I'd be off like a shot,' said Sunil, 'if my dad hit me like that.'

'You don't know though, do you?' said Brad. 'Everyone thinks they know how they'd react in situations but, when it comes down to it, you just don't know. I get the feeling that Col feels sort of responsible for his dad.'

Still, it was worrying, Brad thought, as he left Sunil and headed up to his house. He hoped this latest outburst hadn't got anything to do with him borrowing the Game-Scan. Probably not. He hadn't had it long and Mr Rattersby would have been on the phone yelling and swearing, if he'd noticed it was missing. But Brad made a mental note to return it soon. Best not to take any chances, under the circumstances.

If not the Game-Scan, then maybe it was something to do with Colford himself, Brad reflected. Maybe he'd rattled his dad in some way. It wasn't difficult to upset parents. But somehow, Mr Rattersby didn't seem the type to go ballistic about the things other parents got uptight about. Dirty socks on the living-room floor or toothpaste in the sink. In fact, as far as Brad could make out, it was Colford who did any tidying up. Colford who kept the place from becoming a complete health hazard.

More likely, the outburst was simply a result of a particularly heavy binge. Hopefully another isolated incident. He decided to give Colford a ring, anyway. Just to see how things were.

'I'm fine,' said Colford. 'Yes. Honest. At the moment? Playing this new game I've bought. "Trenches". First World War. You start as a Private and you can work your way right up to General, if you don't get blown up along the way. It's great with the Blast-Pac. No. I can't come round.'

Colford's voice dropped to a whisper.

'Come over here, if you like. Tomorrow night. But not before eight.'

Brad left it till 8.45 before leaving the house on Saturday night. Just to be on the safe side. Had he been lured by the prospect of a new game, was he going out of genuine concern for Colford or was it simply that he had nothing better to do with Sunil out with Gail and Stacey staying home, crying?

Motives didn't matter. As soon as he got there, he knew he'd done the right thing. Colford was gushingly pleased to see him.

It was a bit unnerving. Col was wearing the uniform again. Brad decided against mentioning it. Maybe Col was just entering into the spirit of the game he was loading up. And, apart from the uniform, he looked quite normal. Cheerful, almost.

'You have first go with the Pac, Brad,' he said, handing over the Pac and the 3D visor.

'I've brought my own visor,' Brad said, delving into his bag. 'So we can both play. And I've brought the Game-Scan back. It works fine ... on my machine anyway.'

'Great,' said Colford, though without real enthusiasm. 'We could give it a go, later. Let's start the game, though. It's dead good. I reckon I'm gonna join the army, when I leave school. Be a soldier, like Charles Merrick.'

Brad somehow thought the army wouldn't be right for Col but he didn't say anything. Why spoil whatever fantasies he had? He'd probably grow out of them. And besides, it was obvious Col was keen to start playing.

Brad chose to start as a Private at the Battle of the Somme. The week before the advance, bombarding the enemy lines with artillery fire.

'Go for it, Brad,' Colford encouraged. 'Zap 'em.'

'You can't say that. Not with this game,' said Brad, pausing for a moment. 'Certainly not dressed in that uniform. This is the trenches. You've got to use the right lingo.'

'The what?'

'Lingo. Language. Slang. You have to say... Watch out for that toffee apple, man, or you'll get a blighty one.'

'What?' said Colford, giggling.

'It means watch out for that mortar bomb or you'll get blown to bits,' said Brad. 'You'll be doing all that in history soon.'

'We've started already,' said Colford. 'It's brill. Better than that boring stuff about spinning machines or something.'

'Industrial Revolution,' said Brad, knowingly. 'It's OK but yeah, the First World War's better... Do you have Miss Jackson?'

Colford nodded.

'You'll really love it then,' Brad confirmed. 'You get to watch these great videos and she reads you poems and tells you First World War jokes.'

The jokes, of course, would be wasted on Col but he'd probably enjoy the rest.

'I'm looking forward to doing about the tanks and guns and stuff,' Colford said. ''Cos I'm not usually very good at history but I know a lot about guns. I'll probably do it as my project. Miss Jackson said we'll be able to pick anything we want.'

'Great,' said Brad. 'Hey, you'll have to ask your dad if you can take that uniform in and some of that war stuff from the shed. Miss Jackson'd be dead impressed.'

'No,' said Colford, hastily. 'Dad wouldn't let me. And don't you go letting on you know about it. Don't tell him about me wearing this.'

'I won't,' said Brad. 'I haven't. And neither has Sunil. Come on, let's get on with the game.'

'I'm gonna be Charles Merrick,' said Colford.

'Sorry?'

'You can give your characters names,' Colford explained. 'I'm always Charles. You can be Sam Burton, the gamekeeper's son.'

'Thanks!'

'Yeah,' said Col. ''Cos he was sort of nice, like you. Dead brave. Won the Victoria Cross for helping soldiers under fire.'

Brad wasn't sure he wanted to join Colford's group of heroes. But maybe it was too late to start worrying about that. Maybe it was better not to think too much. Just play the game.

They took it in turns to use the Pac. With that and the 3D visor, it was incredible. And so educational, even his mother might approve, Brad thought. You were right in there, in the trenches, going over the top to the burst of artillery fire, blinded by smoky mist, never knowing what hit you.

'It's not fair,' Colford said, after he'd been killed, like the real Charles. 'You can't win. Whatever you do, you end up losing loads of men and get nowhere.'

'That's the whole point about trench warfare,' Brad pointed out. 'They lost twenty thousand men on the first day of the Somme and managed to advance about a mile!'

'Let's try another section,' said Colford. 'I'm sick of the Somme.'

If only it had been so easy in real life, Brad thought, as Col flicked back to the game menu. I'm sick of the Somme! How many men had said that before they were blasted to fragments, caught up in the nastiest game of them all.

'Hey,' said Colford. 'This section looks good. Firing Squad. I haven't tried that yet.'

First the choice. Game for two players. You could be Soldier A or Soldier B. Choose and enter your names.

'We can't be Sam or Charles any more,' said Brad. 'This is about cowardice, desertion, I reckon. Neither of them were cowards, were they? So who shall we be now?'

'Just say Brad and Col,' said Colford, too anxious to get on with the game to trouble his imagination.

Lying on their stomachs in a trench. Silence, except for the background hum of someone singing to themselves. No guns. No artillery bursts. Spookily, eerily calm.

'All quiet on the Western Front,' whispered Brad.

'What?' said Colford.

'You two lazy blighters,' came the sound of the game voice. 'You're supposed to be part of the patrol. What are you doing here? Out you go or you'll have me to answer to.'

Warily climbing over the parapet. Walking slowly, looking round. Ever cautious. Where were the rest of the patrol? Were they supposed to catch them up? Where were they supposed to be patrolling and why?

Brad wondered whether the confusion was part of the game. Had the real soldiers felt that way? Maybe their orders, their instructions hadn't always been clear.

Walking on through No-Man's-Land because you didn't know what else to do. Coming to the crater. Vast and wide but shallow, all the same.

'Down,' Colford hissed.

Col had seen them first but Brad's reactions were quicker. He dropped flat to the ground as the enemy opened fire, blasting Col's character, which twitched and jolted in spasms on the ground. Brad didn't turn to look how the real Col was reacting. Didn't see him bashing at the controls in frustration that his part in all this was over.

Brad was totally absorbed, slithering backwards on his belly. Not even bothering to pick up the rifle he'd dropped as he fell. Desperate to get back to the trench. He knew instinctively what he had to do. Warn the others of the impending attack.

He never made it. Suddenly the scene switched. No longer in the field but in a makeshift court room. A military court room.

CHAPTER SIXTEEN

'Soldier,' said the game voice. 'You are charged with desertion and of casting away your weapon in the face of the enemy. How do you plead?'

'Hey!' said Brad, swinging round to face Col. 'That's not fair! I wasn't deserting. I was going back to warn them!'

'Plead Not Guilty then,' said Col, logically.

'This is stupid,' said Brad, as the court rejected his plea and condemned him anyway. 'I'm not playing!' he added, as the scene automatically changed once again.

'Oh, go on, Brad,' said Col, excitedly, as he saw the firing squad. 'I want to see what happens.'

'I get shot, that's what happens!' said Brad.

'Your character gets shot,' Colford pointed out. 'Go on, it'll be great. You've got the Blast-Pac!'

'No,' said Brad.

He didn't know why he'd refused. He... or his characters... had been shot in hundreds of games before. He'd died in space, in the Core, in car crashes and under the sea. But he wasn't going to die here. Not like this. Because he wasn't a coward. Not even a virtual coward. And it wasn't fair!

'I know,' said Col. 'I'll do it. I'll be you. You can do the shooting.'

'I don't want to shoot you,' said Brad, petulantly.

Col stared at him, sulky disappointment settling on his face, as if someone refusing to shoot you was some sort of desperate insult.

'I know,' said Brad. 'We'll use the Game-Scan. I'll show you how it works and we'll scan in someone we really hate, eh? Now who can we think of..?' he added, quickly fixing up the Scan.

'My dad,' said Colford. 'There'll be a photo of him around somewhere.'

The answer took Brad by surprise. Partly because Col had always been so supportive, so defensive of his dad, and partly because it had been a rhetorical question, anyway. He had the perfect candidate in mind already.

'You don't want to kill your dad!' Brad informed Colford. 'Besides I've got something here.'

He picked up his jacket, which he'd dumped on the floor, and pulled a photograph out of the pocket.

'That's Phil!' said Colford. 'Stacey's boyfriend.'

'Ex-boyfriend,' said Brad. 'Soon to be very ex! Dead. Kaput.'

He scanned in the photograph and within seconds Phil's smarmy face appeared, filling the screen.

'That don't look right,' said Colford.

'It isn't,' said Brad. 'We just have to get it to size, look, and fit it to the character we want. There!'

'Wow,' squeaked Col, excitedly, as the soldier with his back to the wall took on the familiar features. 'That's brill. Now we can both do the shooting.'

'This really happened, you know, Col,' said Brad, a bit

unnerved by Colford's eagerness.

'What did?'

'Soldiers getting shot for desertion and cowardice. The Brits killed 268 of their own men.'

'How do you know?' said Col. 'How do you remember stuff like that?'

'Miss Jackson told us. It sort of stuck in my mind. 'Cos she read us a couple of the Merrick letters too. You know, the ones Charles wrote to his father?'

'Yeah. I know about those,' said Colford. 'Mr Merrick told me.'

Oh, boy, thought Brad, here we go again!

'Er . . . right,' said Brad. 'And did he tell you about the bloke called Jones, who got shot for desertion, though it was obvious he was sick? Shell-shocked. He might not even have intended to desert. Like me, in the game. It could have been a mistake. An accident.'

'Yeah, he told me all that,' said Colford. 'Because poor Charles had nightmares about it. He said so in his letters, just before he was killed at the Somme. Mr Merrick never really got over that. He did all sorts of things after the war. Charity stuff to help other families and shell-shocked soldiers. Set up a trust in Charles's name.'

'That's right,' said Brad. 'But how come you know all that, if you've only just started the war topic? Miss Jackson doesn't usually get onto Merrick till near the end.'

'She didn't tell me,' said Colford, slightly exasperated. 'Mr Merrick did.'

Brad sighed. This was getting seriously weird.

Obviously Colford had read the copies of the letters in the library or something. That's how he knew. But then, Col had never been a great one for reading. He still went to Learning Support for extra help so there was no way he could have researched something like that for himself. No way at all. So Miss Jackson must have told him. She must have!

'Mr Merrick loved Charles so much,' said Colford. 'He never shouted at him or hit him, you know.'

'Didn't he?' said Brad, with a fair idea of where this particular fantasy was coming from.

'No. And he says my dad shouldn't hit me either.'

'Well, no, he shouldn't really,' said Brad, nervously.

He'd told Col often enough to talk about his problems, but now Col was opening up, Brad wasn't at all sure what to say.

'And if it keeps happening,' Brad went on, 'you have to tell your social worker or someone. You have to tell them the truth. You know that, don't you, Col?'

Colford hunched up on his seat and shook his head. Over and over.

'Mr Merrick talks about Charles a lot,' said Col, changing the subject, talking in short, neurotic bursts. 'He's ever so proud of him. Always was. Loved him to bits. Of course, they're together again now, which is nice. That's what happens when you die. Everything's nice again.'

Brad shuddered. He knew it was all made-up gibber but he just couldn't help it. With the dim lighting and Col sitting there in that uniform, talking about dying, it was creepy. Seriously creepy.

What was he supposed to say? What was he supposed to do?

'Sure, Col,' he said, knowing he was copping out. 'Come on. Let's play, eh?'

He knew he should have tried to talk to Col. Draw him out a bit further. But somehow he couldn't. He didn't want to think about reality. About Col's problems and his crazy fantasies. About Merrick. About the war. About all the young men who died. About their families, reading the letters.

He just wanted to lose himself in the game, especially with Phil's face, still on the screen, temptingly smug.

'Ready.'

This was Phil standing there, not a real soldier in a real war.

'Aim.'

Not even the real Phil, for heaven's sake. A virtual Phil. A harmless fantasy. Like Col's talking statue. A game.

'Fire.'

Brad screamed out, as the blast ripping through his back caught him totally by surprise.

Stupid, stupid, stupid! He'd forgotten he was still wearing the Pac. Forgotten he was still Soldier A, no matter whose face you scanned in. It wasn't Phil he'd blasted. It was himself!

Brad's back was still tingling, when the phone rang.

'Yes, Mr Bradshaw,' said Colford into the receiver. 'Yes, he is. I'll ask him. Brad, do you know what time it is?'

'Oh, heck, it's nearly midnight,' said Brad, looking at his watch.

'It's nearly midnight, Mr Bradshaw,' Colford repeated.

'I know that!' Brad heard his father yell down the phone. 'And he was supposed to be home an hour ago!'

'Tell him I'm on my way,' said Brad, removing his Pac and visor.

As Brad stood up to leave, the boys heard the scream of tyres outside, the banging of a car door, the slamming of the gate.

'He's early,' said Colford, looking anxiously down at his uniform. 'Go out the back, Brad.'

But it was too late. Mr Rattersby had burst in.

'What the hell are you doing in that uniform?' he yelled. 'And what's he doing round here again, snooping?'

There was no gun this time but Mr Rattersby looked wilder, more dangerous, than he'd done before, on the night of the leaky ceiling.

Brad wasn't sure what to do. He didn't want to provoke the man further but how could he leave Colford here with him alone, under the circumstances?

'You'd better go, Brad,' Colford hissed at him. 'Please.'

'It's OK,' Brad said to Mr Rattersby, edging round his large frame. 'We weren't doing anything. Just playing.'

He bolted out, grabbing his bike, which he'd left on the side path. As he pushed it towards the gate, he heard Colford cry out. Again and again.

Brad looked around wildly at the neighbouring cottages. All the lights were off. Most of the residents were elderly and went to bed early. Should he go back in? Could he even get back in? He was sure he'd heard the door being bolted behind him.

But he couldn't simply go home. He had to get help. He felt in his pocket for his mobile. It wasn't there. He abandoned the bike and ran across the road to the house of someone he knew. He banged on the door and waited.

He felt a bit foolish when Mr Morris appeared in his pyjamas. Colford's cottage had gone quiet. Maybe everything was OK. Maybe he was over-reacting.

'I think,' he said hesitantly, 'there's something going on, over at the Rattersbys'.'

'Usually is,' said Mr Morris, opening the door wide, letting him in.

'I don't know whether I ought to phone the police,' said Brad. 'I don't know what's happening. Mr Rattersby came in drunk and I heard him hitting Colford and . . .'

'Aye, well we'd better phone the police, then,' said Mr Morris. 'Not that it will do any good. But it won't do any harm, either.'

But it did. On Monday at school Colford refused to speak to Brad. Even to look at him. As Mr Morris had predicted, the police had been unable to do anything. The drama, whatever it was, was over by the time they arrived. Both Colford and Mr Rattersby swore nothing had happened.

Brad sought out Stacey, partly because he thought she'd want to know and partly because he just needed to talk.

'I don't understand Col,' Stacey said, momentarily distracted from her own problems. 'I mean, what did he expect you to do? Walk away and let him get beaten to pulp?'

'I think that's exactly what he expected... what he wanted me to do. Col doesn't see it the way we do. He's got so used to the violence over the years, I swear he thinks it's normal. I bet Col's mum used to get knocked around too. I bet that's why she left.'

'Maybe she didn't leave,' said Stacey. 'For all we know, she could be buried in the back garden. And Col could be next! Then perhaps someone'll do something about it. Honestly, social services make me sick.'

'Yeah, but they can't win, can they?' said Brad. 'Whatever they do or don't do. And with someone Col's age, it's tricky. If he doesn't want to go.'

'But why? He'd be better off almost anywhere,' said Stacey, echoing what Sunil had said.

'That's what we all think. But we're not seeing it from Col's point of view, are we? His dad may be a violent, drunken slob but he's all Col's got. And Col manages most of the time. I guess you put up with quite a lot if you love someone enough.'

Bad move that. The very mention of love started Stacey off snivelling, hurling her back into her own pit of depression.

Brad couldn't really understand it. He'd been pretty cut up when he and Stacey had split up. Had stamped around snarling at everyone for weeks. He'd even cried a bit. But not in public. Not out in the playground. Not all day, every day, like this. And you couldn't just dismiss it as a gender difference either. Emma never went on like this, when she got dumped.

'I'm sorry,' Stacey said. 'It's not fair, me carrying on like this. Not in front of you.'

'It's OK,' said Brad, shrugging.

'It's just that I got so involved so quickly. It was so intense. I thought it was going so well. He said I was special. Different to all the others. He said . . . he said he loved me.'

Brad could have pointed out that Stacey had once said the same thing to him. That words were cheap. That Phil simply wasn't capable of loving anyone except himself. But he didn't. He couldn't bear to see Stacey so upset. Wouldn't dream of making it worse.

'And I don't know what went wrong,' she snivelled. 'I don't know what I've done.'

'Nothing,' said Brad, trying not to get exasperated. 'You wouldn't have to do anything. Just like Col probably doesn't have to do anything to make his dad start on him. I guess some people just get their kicks from hurting others.'

'Phil's not like that,' said Stacey, setting off in full flood again.

She'd been completely brainwashed, Brad thought. How could anyone be so taken in by a serial philanderer? Unless . . . A horrible thought struck him. All this crying. All this raw emotion. It was too intense for someone who'd simply been dumped. What if there was something else behind it? What if Stacey had been so besotted by Phil that she'd..? He couldn't help it. It came straight out, before he had time to think.

'Stacey,' he said. 'You're not pregnant, are you?'

'Pregnant?' she said, glaring at him. 'What sort of idiot do you take me for, Brad?'

'Er... I don't. I just thought...'

'Well, don't,' she snapped. 'Think about something else. Think about Col. What are we going to do about him?'

CHAPTER SEVENTEEN

Brad and Sunil were late for registration. Colford hadn't been on the school bus again. He'd been in school on Monday, missed Tuesday, turned up Wednesday looking more withdrawn and miserable than ever, missed Thursday and now he was missing again.

Stacey had decided that, as Brad knew Colford best, he ought to have a word with the Year 9 tutor. Brad had taken Sunil with him for support. He'd explained to the tutor how he'd tried to phone Colford several times over the last few days and only got the answering machine. He'd asked the tutor to look into it, without mentioning Brad's name. Colford wouldn't appreciate him interfering again.

It was doubtful, anyway, if the Year tutor would do anything.

'We'll give it till Monday,' he'd said. 'Colford's social worker's coming in again on Monday. We're doing what we can.'

There was something in the tutor's voice which had hinted it was none of Brad's business anyway. Maybe it wasn't but he couldn't help worrying. He and Sunil left the main building and went round the back to the humanities block where all the Year 10s registered. Hovering by the door, with his electronic note pad, was a prefect. Not just any prefect either.

'Can you sign in, please,' said Phil. 'You're late.'

Sunil took the pad and tapped in his number.

'We're not late,' said Brad, pushing past them. 'We've been to see someone.'

'You're still late,' said Phil, following him inside and halfway up the stairs. 'Registers have been done, so you've got to check in. What's your number? I'll do it for you.'

'Can't remember.'

'Don't be stupid, Brad. It's nearly time for the bell. If you don't check in I'll have to report you.'

'So, do it, then.'

'Come on, Brad,' said Sunil, catching up with him, whispering in his ear. 'What's the point of being awkward?'

He *was* being awkward. Deliberately awkward. Stupid, childish, belligerent. He didn't care. He'd rather have a detention than have Philandering Phil telling him what to do.

'This isn't about registering, is it?' said Phil, with that stupid smirk on his face. 'It wasn't my fault Stacey dumped you, you know.'

Sunil held Brad back as he tried to lurch forward.

'Don't be an idiot,' Sunil hissed. 'Just register.'

Sunil took the pad from Phil and started to enter Brad's number. Brad snatched it from him and dropped it deliberately onto the floor.

'Pick it up,' Phil said.

'Pick it up yourself,' Brad snarled.

'Cut it out, you two,' said Sunil, picking up the pad. 'This is pathetic.'

He positioned himself between the two snarling opponents. A tricky manoeuvre in itself, as they were halfway up the stairs. Still trickier because he had to keep away from Brad long enough to enter his number.

'There,' Sunil said, triumphantly. 'Done. Now come on!'

Brad was just about to move, reluctantly, upwards towards their classroom on the first floor, when the door at the bottom of the stairs swung open and slammed shut again with a loud bang.

All three of them looked at the figure standing by the now closed door, blocking the exit.

'Oh, no,' Brad said.

It was Colford. And he was wearing his uniform. His First World War uniform. Complete with rifle.

Three thoughts passed through Brad's mind as Sunil and Phil bunched up close next to him. Three attempts to grasp at half reasonable explanations. One was that Colford's class had history first lesson. That Col had taken up Brad's suggestion to bring some of his stuff in and was on his way to the history room, specially kitted out.

The second was that Colford had simply got so attached to the flaming uniform that he'd taken to wearing it permanently. The third was that Col had got his dates mixed up. Next Friday was one of their mufti days, when for a small donation to charity you could wear what you liked. Most people came in casual stuff but some chose fancy dress or coated themselves in tons of weird and wonderful make-up.

'What you doing then, Col?' he asked, moving down a

couple of steps. 'Mufti day's not till next week, you know.'

Colford, he noticed, was deadly pale. Very twitchy. Even more hunched and neurotic-looking than usual.

'Watch it,' hissed Phil, as Colford raised the rifle.

Brad half turned and gave him a withering look.

'It's a replica, pea-brain,' he said. 'Col's playing. Getting into the role.'

'No,' said Colford.

'Oh, heck,' said Brad, starting to panic a bit. 'You haven't brought a real rifle into school! Even if it's for history! Col, you'll get yourself excluded! I hope it's not loaded.'

'No,' said Colford.

Was that no, it wasn't loaded or no, it is?

Brad felt someone's hand, maybe Sunil's, maybe Phil's, grab the back of his jacket, trying to hold him back as he moved down another step. Was it that gesture which alerted him to a sudden sense of danger? Or was it Colford's eyes, wide and watery? Or the manic tone as he spoke?

'He shouldn't have done it,' Colford said. 'He shouldn't have done it.'

'Who?' said Brad, trying to relax his facial muscles into a smile. 'What you on about, Col?'

'He shouldn't have done it,' Colford repeated. 'He shouldn't have kept doing it. It wasn't right, was it? I told him it wasn't right. He should have loved me, like Mr Merrick loved Charles. I told him, Mr Merrick said it wasn't right. Don't move!'

138

Brad felt his body stiffen and freeze, though he guessed the instruction wasn't aimed at him. He'd been aware of very light footsteps behind him. He hadn't dared look round but guessed that either Phil or Sunil was trying to make his way upstairs to alert one of the teachers. They were over-reacting, of course. Poor Col wasn't dangerous. Just a bit worked up over something.

Brad wanted to look at his watch but didn't want to make any sudden movements. He wasn't scared but there was no point spooking Colford. It must nearly be the end of registration. Any second now, the bell would go. People would come flooding out of the room next to where Colford was standing. Others would come stampeding downstairs or bursting in from outside.

There wasn't any real danger, as such, Brad kept telling himself. The rifle, even if real, wouldn't be loaded. But Col would be in dead trouble if anyone else saw him with it. So priority was to get Col calmed down and out of the way before that happened. Then Brad would have to grovel to Phil. To get him to keep his big prefect, holier-than-thou mouth shut.

'All right, Col,' Brad said, in what he hoped was a cheery, normal sort of voice. 'Nobody's moving. Calm down. What's all this about?'

'I told him,' Colford said, shaking his head. 'I wasn't harming his stuff. I was only playing. He shouldn't have gone on at me. He shouldn't have kept doing it.'

'He's flipped. He's completely out of it,' Brad heard Sunil whisper.

'He's OK,' Brad whispered back, more to reassure himself than the other two. 'It's your dad, yeah?' he said, quickly dropping down onto the bottom step, feeling the others bunched on the step above him.

'He shouldn't have done it,' Colford repeated, starting to cry. 'Not again. I told him. It wasn't fair. I loved him.'

Past tense.

'I loved him. I didn't do it. It wasn't meant to happen. It was an accident.'

'What the hell have you done?' Phil's voice burst out, unnaturally high and squeaky.

Brad wanted to swing round and punch him in the mouth. What did Phil know? What did he understand? Col hadn't done anything. He couldn't have done. His dad had had a go at him again. He'd got himself into a state, that was all. Gibbering nonsense.

'I've told Mr Merrick,' said Colford. 'I told him what I'd done. He said it was OK. An accident, he said. Not my fault. Not my fault. Not my fault.'

'Hey, Col,' Brad said, edging forward. 'Come on. It's OK. Whatever you've done, it'll be OK.'

He saw the rifle being raised. Heard the click.

He still felt strangely calm. Felt no sense of personal danger. The only problem was if that blasted bell went before he could get Colford out of there.

'They were going to take me away,' Colford said. 'I warned my dad. They were going to put me in care again. If he kept doing it. But he didn't love me like Mr

Merrick loved Charles. He didn't care. He didn't care if the social workers came.'

Suddenly Colford's glazed vacant look changed as he focused on Brad.

'You sent them, Brad,' he added, accusingly. 'You let me down. You told them to take me away.'

'No,' said Brad.

In that moment the realization hit. The rifle was real. It was loaded. Sunil was right. Colford had completely flipped. He wasn't rational. Wasn't in control.

'Don't move,' Colford said again, as Phil sidled down, positioning himself next to Brad on the bottom step.

Somehow Phil didn't seem, to Brad, to be the type to go in for heroics. He hoped he was right. At this distance Col couldn't miss.

Overhead came the sound of chairs being pulled back and the shuffling of feet, in preparation for the bell which only a second later started to ring. To their right, a classroom door burst open, drawing all eyes but Colford's. Three girls pushed through in a heap, then froze, mid-action, like some bizarre cartoon as they saw Colford. Stacey, Emma and Paula looked towards Brad and beyond him to the stairs where more pupils had gathered. Their initial shouts and giggles quickly fell silent.

'Come on,' a teacher's voice bellowed from the top. 'Get a move on. What's the hold-up?'

They'd all read about shootings in schools. Most had recently attended the video-games debate, where all the gory details had been spewed out for discussion. But it was something which happened to other people, in other schools, in rough areas. Not here, in the middle of the countryside with a kid you knew wearing a First World War uniform, holding a rifle in white, trembling hands.

Brad couldn't turn round. He could only guess by the sound of nervous shuffling, followed by quiet, though firm footsteps that the wave of pupils had parted to make way for the teacher. A fact confirmed by the growing agitation on Colford's face, the rapid flickering of the eyelids. There was no knowing what was going on in anyone else's mind. The whole situation was explosive. Unpredictable. The teacher, Mr Purcell, by the sound of his voice, took momentary control.

'We're all going to move quietly back into the classrooms,' he said, in a calm but firm tone. 'OK, people at the top of the stairs, move back please.'

It was all credit to Mr Purcell that there was no stampeding panic. Brad could sense the immediate obedience of those behind him and saw the slight nod of Emma's head as the girls began to retreat to comparative safety.

Colford seemed relieved. Seemed even to relax slightly, though still keeping the gun raised. Mr Purcell had been right. Retreating not advancing was the best strategy. Brad waited a couple of seconds until he was sure the way behind him was clear. Then he intended to back up.

Too late. Through the glass doors, behind Colford, he could see kids swarming forward. They'd only see Colford's back. They were chatting, giggling, swinging their bags at one another. They wouldn't clock what was going on. They'd burst in. Col would panic. Brad put his hands up slightly in a reassuring gesture of surrender.

'Col,' he said.

At that moment the door swung open and four kids piled through at once, almost crashing into Colford whose fingers pressed down on the trigger.

Brad felt the world go into slow motion. His body, no longer part of him, seemed to lift into the air before he felt the impact. Before everything went black.

CHAPTER EIGHTEEN

1917

Barnaby Merrick left the house and strode out across the lawn. It was early afternoon but time had no meaning any more. It was an incredibly warm day, for October, but he barely noticed. Sometimes he just had to get out. Day or night, rain or shine. Walk for miles until he was exhausted. It was the only way to induce sleep.

Maybe he'd done the wrong thing, he thought. Opening up the house as a military hospital and convalescent home for wounded soldiers. He'd moved into four isolated rooms in the West Wing but they weren't remote enough to block out the constant scurrying of doctors and nurses. The screams in the night.

Across the lawn, under the large oak where Charles and little Sam Burton had once played, lay a blanket. On the blanket were stretched two young men. One with his face completely bandaged, showing only the mouth and eyes. The other, an attractive young lad with blond hair, delicately sculptured features and dull, glazed eyes which no longer saw. The doctors could find nothing physically wrong. The boy wasn't actually blind. His brain had somehow shut down. He simply refused to see.

'Malingering,' someone had muttered. 'So he won't get sent back to the front.'

But Barnaby didn't think the young lad was putting it on. Who knew what those eyes had once witnessed? Who could say what he was blotting out?

Beside the blanket were two wheelchairs. Two lads who would never walk again. One of them Barnaby knew well. Bertie. Bertie had a look of Charles about him, which is why Barnaby had first picked him out. The dark hair, the same ever-questioning brown eyes.

Barnaby had been there when Bertie's parents had come for their first and only visit. He'd seen the mother break down in tears as Bertie tried to speak, mouthing only a jumble of confused sounds, as spit dribbled down the side of his mouth. It wasn't only his legs he had lost. Physically he was as helpless as a baby. But his mind was intact. He knew what was going on.

Barnaby had stared, aghast, as Bertie's father walked away. He'd rushed after him, grabbed his arm.

'You can't do that!' he'd said. 'You can't just walk away. He's not a cabbage. He might not be able to speak but he knows what's going on. He needs you.'

The man pulled his arm away, shook his head and walked on without looking back.

'He's alive!' Barnaby had called after him. 'At least your son's alive.'

And so they all were. These constant reminders of what he had lost. Of what they themselves had lost. He lived with the constant torment of watching them. But what could he do?

He'd had to do something. It wasn't only him who had suffered. Almost all the workers on the estate had lost someone. Burton had lost three of his sons. Only young Sam had survived. And who knew for how much longer he would go on surviving out there?

Barnaby hurried across the lawn and out towards the woods.

145

Some days he stayed to talk to the wounded soldiers. On others, he found it unbearable. He needed to be alone. He strode on, trying to absorb the peace and tranquillity, to draw it into himself like a parched man, desperately sucking water through a straw.

The sound of the shot stopped him. He paused and listened. All shooting had been banned on the estate. The slightest noise could set the men off. Even the doors of the house had been fitted with strips of rubber to prevent them banging. He listened a while longer. Nothing. Just that single shot.

As he walked on a figure came crashing through the trees in front of him. A figure wearing pyjamas, his head bandaged and in his right hand a revolver. Where the hell had he got that from? Whatever weapons were around were in a securely locked cabinet, in an office. Or they were supposed to be.

The figure froze for a moment. Barnaby searched in his mind, trying to fit a name to the face. Lonegan. Jim Lonegan. One of the psychiatric cases. One who was supposed to be constantly under watch.

'Fall back,' Jim shouted. 'Fall back. They've broken through our lines.'

'It's all right,' Barnaby said, stretching out his hand. 'It's all right. Give me the gun. I'll hold them off.'

Against all Barnaby's expectations, Jim handed over the gun and fell to his knees, sobbing, clutching hold of Barnaby.

'I didn't run away,' he sobbed. 'I got him. I didn't run away.'

They were still there a moment later, when Jane Burton appeared.

'Oh, sir. Mr Merrick,' she cried out. 'Come quickly. There's been an accident. It's Father.'

She looked from Barnaby's face to the gun in his hand. She saw the young man, kneeling on the ground, sobbing. Knew it was no accident.

'Run up to the Hall, Jane,' said Barnaby, holding onto the young man, unable to move. 'Get help.'

Burton was taken back to the Hall. He was going to be all right. He'd surprised Jim in the woods. Been hit in the leg, as Jim fired in panic, taking him for a German. Burton would be fine, thank God, but he'd insisted on seeing Barnaby before he'd let anyone treat the injury.

'Don't let them press charges against the lad,' he'd urged. 'It was an accident. The gun went off accidentally. He didn't mean to hurt me. It was an accident. Do you understand?'

Barnaby understood. Just as Burton had done. Jim Lonegan was a kid. Barely turned eighteen when he'd been dragged from a water-logged shell hole at Passchendaele. In his mind, Jim was still there. Forever hearing the artillery bursts which shattered his brain, still seeing his mates being blown to pieces, still fighting the enemy.

It was all a tragic accident, as Barnaby told the young woman reporter who turned up later, one of the many young women who'd taken on unfamiliar jobs. She'd done well. Asked all the right questions. It was just the answers which were difficult.

'The lad managed to slip out while his nurse was attending to someone else,' Barnaby had told her. 'No, he wasn't locked in . . . No, we don't know how he managed to get his hands on the gun. . . Yes, there'll be an enquiry. . . Yes, they would learn from their mistakes. . . No, the general public aren't at risk from our patients.'

He'd led her into the small sitting room at the back of the house.

'These are the ones at risk,' he'd said, pointing out a small group by the window, playing cards. 'These are the lads who've been passed fit to serve. A week or so and they'll all be back on the front line.'

'Let's hope it will be over soon,' the young woman had muttered.

'Ah, yes, hope,' repeated Barnaby. 'That's all we've really got left, isn't it?'

CHAPTER NINETEEN

Brad rubbed his eyes and looked again at the closely printed document in front of him. He was sitting at a small table in the corner of the library. The same table he'd been sitting at every lunch break since his return to school.

He looked up, vaguely aware of a figure hovering over him.

'Hi,' said Stacey, pulling out a chair and sitting beside him.

She glanced at the letter he was reading. At the rest of the Merrick papers scattered around the table.

'Why?' she said with an expression which was part smile and part frown. 'Why are you reading all this stuff?'

'I don't know,' said Brad. 'Looking for answers, maybe.'

'You've got to snap out of this, you know, Brad,' said Stacey gently. 'None of it was your fault.'

'I'm OK,' said Brad. 'Honest.'

'So that's why you lock yourself away up here, with Barnaby Merrick's paperwork, is it? That's why you've stopped going out. That's why you barely speak to anyone these days. Because you're OK?'

'I'm fine. It's just . . .'

Brad paused. It was impossible to explain. Even to himself. It was like he was no longer living in the present. As if he'd been caught in some sort of time warp. As if time had frozen around him two months ago, refusing to let him free. Condemning him to think, analyse, re-live every second. Re-play every conversation in his head. See the images float ceaselessly in front of his eyes. Endure the incident over and over. The incident, people assured him, which could have been much worse...

The bullet had only nicked his shoulder. He'd broken his wrist and suffered mild concussion as his head smashed into the wall. The wall Phil had pushed him into, breaking his own ankle in the process, as he fell from the stairs.

Phil, the school hero. Phil, who had probably saved Brad's life. So yes, for him, for the other kids who were in the humanities block that day, it could have been much worse. But not for Colford. Or Colford's dad.

The police had found Mr Rattersby lying on the floor of the shed. A single, fatal bullet wound to his chest.

'It was an accident,' Colford had later claimed to the police. 'I was playing in the shed, with the uniform and stuff. He came in. He started yelling at me again. He came at me. The gun went off. I couldn't help it. It just went off. I didn't want to kill him. I didn't. I didn't. I loved him. He was my dad.'

'Brad?' Stacey said. 'Brad? Are you OK? You've gone white. Absolutely white. Come on. Pack this stuff away. We'll go outside.'

Brad didn't argue. He let Stacey pack up and hand the papers back to the librarian. He followed her out of the library and down the stairs, barely knowing what he was doing or where he was going.

In his mind, he was back in that hospital room. Two

police officers by his bedside. Asking questions. Expecting him to know the answers. How well did he know Colford? Did Colford have a particular grudge against him? Had Colford spoken much about his father? Had he ever mentioned wanting to kill him?

To the police it had all seemed callous, pre-meditated. The way Col was dressed in that uniform. The single, deadly shot. The way he'd left his dad lying there and cycled into school. More threats. More gun waving.

'No,' Brad had insisted. 'It wasn't like that. Col didn't mean to harm anyone. He couldn't have done. It was all an accident. It must have been. I know Col was a bit strange sometimes but...'

The police had picked up on that word, 'strange', and Brad had found himself explaining about Col's obsession with Merrick. Condemning Colford with every word.

'Sit down for a minute,' Stacey ordered, catapulting Brad back into the present. 'And take some deep breaths.'

Brad flopped down onto the low wall in front of the drama studio, where Stacey had led him.

'Come on, Brad,' she urged. 'Deep breaths or you're going to pass out on me.'

Strange, Brad thought, as his head spun round and round, how a simple matter like breathing could suddenly become so difficult. Especially in the middle of the night when he'd wake up sweating, choking. His parents dashing in, in response to screams he didn't know he'd made.

'I think I'm cracking up, Stacey,' said Brad, his head down to hide the tears. 'Like Col. My head's a mess. I

151

keep going over everything again and again. Seeing Colford every minute of the day. Colford in that bloody uniform. Colford doing what he did. He's still having the tests, you know. Psychiatric tests! Probing. Dissecting every minute of his miserable existence.'

'I know,' said Stacey, reaching out to touch Brad's hand. 'But it's for the best, Brad. Really, it is. If they can prove Col wasn't responsible for his actions ...'

'If they can prove he's mad, you mean?'

'No,' said Stacey. 'Not mad. Just unstable ... because of his circumstances. He'll get help, Brad. He'll finally get the help and support he needs.'

'Finally,' said Brad, looking up, no longer caring about the tears. 'Finally! When it's too late. Why didn't I do something? I knew the violence had started again. I knew Col was cracking up. I'd heard him talking to that statue. I'd seen him in that flaming uniform. I'd even encouraged him! Sat playing "Trenches" with him, like everything was one big, bloody game. Instead of listening to him. Instead of trying to help. Why didn't I stop him? Why didn't I do something?'

'You did,' Stacey pointed out quietly. 'You told your parents. You told Col's tutor. You got the police round that night and they got the social worker in.'

'And Col hated me for it. I messed everything up for him.'

'No, Brad,' said Stacey, almost shouting. 'Col was already in a mess. You did everything right. You know you did. What more could you have done?'

152

'I don't know.'

It was a question Brad had asked himself time and time again, as he listened to all the speculation around the school, in the village, on the bus, in the shops. Everywhere you went, people were still talking about it. It wasn't often anybody got shot round here.

There'd been a drugs-related murder in town seven years ago. A nasty domestic back in the 1960s when a woman had gone berserk, shooting her violent husband, her three kids and then herself.

Then there was the shooting, here at the Hall, which Brad had been reading about in the Merrick papers. When a shell-shocked soldier called Lonegan had taken a pot shot at the gamekeeper, mistaking him for a German spy. The soldier had escaped charges but had received electric shock treatment, on the recommendation of psychiatrists, which just about finished off any brain function he might have had left.

At least, thought Brad, psychiatric care had moved on a bit since those days. Whatever lay in store for Col, it wouldn't be as horrendous as that.

'You're shivering,' said Stacey, putting her arm round him.

Brad winced as she touched his shoulder.

'Sorry,' said Stacey, withdrawing slightly. 'I just wish there was something I could do to help.'

'You are helping,' said Brad. 'Everyone's been trying to help.'

It was true. His parents, his teachers, his friends, even

153

his brother Nick had been really kind and patient. Today was the first time anyone had put pressure on him to 'snap out of it'. Trust it to be Stacey! But she was right. He had to try to move on with his life, before he drove himself crazy.

'Look,' said Stacey, 'I don't want to hassle you and I know it might be a bit soon but I reckon you need to start going out again. Get back into circulation a bit. Why don't you come round tonight? Steve's got this new game he thought you might like to try.'

'I don't know,' said Brad, shrugging.

He hadn't told Stacey, hadn't told anyone in fact, that he hadn't played any video games since the incident. It wasn't a conscious decision. He just couldn't face them. He hadn't even tried. He just knew he couldn't. Like that guy he'd seen on TV recently, who'd been in a serious train crash seventeen years earlier and who, despite hours of counselling, still couldn't travel by rail.

Seventeen years! Could something really haunt you so completely and for so long? Would he always associate the video games with Colford?

Not that Brad thought the games had anything to do with what had happened, though there were many who did. It hadn't taken long for news to spread about what the police had taken away from the Rattersbys' cottage. The Blast-Pac, the Game-Scan, the 3D visor, all the war games, 'Survival' and dozens more like it. People had quickly put two and two together and made 666. The number of the beast!

'What do you expect?' people had muttered. 'When kids sit in front of that muck, day and night?'

Not that the games had been the only target for blame. There were dozens. Even the school had come under scrutiny for its poor security system.

'Brad?' Stacey was saying. 'I've lost you again!'

'Sorry, I was thinking.'

'I could see that!'

'People want easy answers, don't they?' Brad said. 'Only it's too simplistic to blame the social workers or the police or Mr Rattersby or the games...'

'Or yourself,' Stacey added.

'I'm sorry,' said Brad. 'I don't mean to be so...'

'You don't have to apologize for being caring,' said Stacey. 'But you do have to... good heavens, look at that!'

Brad followed the direction of Stacey's eyes towards the back wall of the main building, where Philandering Phil was leaning, whispering in some girl's ear while one of his hands crept up the back of her jumper; the position of his other hand made Brad positively blush.

'Who's he with?' said Brad. 'I don't recognize her. It's certainly not Kara.'

'No,' said Stacey. 'He dumped Kara a while back for Rosie. But that's not Rosie, either. Hang about. I know who it is. It's one of those German exchange students. They only arrived two days ago!'

'Ah,' said Brad. 'That explains it then, doesn't it? He's probably just practising his German.'

'That's not German he's practising!' said Stacey. 'Yuk. I

can't bear to watch. Let's go round the front.'

Brad stood up and let Stacey tuck her arm into his. Relieved, at least, that she seemed repulsed rather than upset by Phil's antics.

'You know, I thought,' Stacey exploded as they hurried round to the front of the main building, 'for one little moment, after Phil pushed you out of the way that day, that maybe we'd all misjudged him. That maybe he had some slight redeeming feature, after all.'

'He does,' said Brad. 'That was brave of him. Genuinely brave. And I'm grateful. Honestly. But where girls are concerned he's still a total shit!'

'Language!' said Stacey, laughing.

Brad smiled at her. It seemed strange. Alien. Not something he'd been used to doing for a while. But it seemed to have a good effect. Stacey beamed back at him.

'Anyway,' she said. 'You still haven't given me an answer. About tonight.'

'I don't know,' said Brad. 'I'm not sure . . .'

'This isn't about me and you,' said Stacey, misunderstanding his reluctance. 'I'm inviting you to try out Steve's game, that's all. I'm not trying to force you back into anything.'

'You wouldn't have to force me,' said Brad.

'What then?' said Stacey. 'What's the problem?'

'I've still got a lot of work to catch up on.'

'I could help you.'

'And . . .'

Brad paused. He still didn't want to admit to his fears

about the games. And maybe it would help, being with other people. Easing himself back into some sort of normality.

'Yeah,' he said, finally making a decision. 'Yeah. I'll come round.'

'Great,' said Stacey, pausing by the statue of Barnaby Merrick, leaning forward and kissing Brad's cheek.

'Hey,' said Sunil, wandering over to join them. 'Are you two back together then?'

'Yes,' said Stacey.

'No,' said Brad at the same time.

'Sort of,' they compromised, as Sunil looked from one to the other.

'Well, maybe you could make your minds up on the way to registration,' he said. 'Bell went five minutes ago. Oh puke, look at him!'

Phil limped past them, supported by the German exchange girl.

'He makes me sick!' said Sunil. 'The way he's still limping around, making a big deal out of his broken ankle. Drawing attention to it. As if his bit of heroism was the only thing that mattered. I don't suppose he ever gives poor Col or Mr Rattersby or anyone else a second thought. It's just self, self, self, with Phil.'

Brad felt the colour drain from his face. The very thought of Colford, the very mention of his name still made him feel sick with guilt, no matter how hard he tried to move on.

He sat down on the base of the statue.

'Are you OK?' said Sunil.

'Yeah. I'm OK. Never got round to having any lunch. I feel a bit faint, that's all. I'll be OK in a minute. You two go on to registration.'

Brad leant back against Barnaby Merrick's marble legs, as Sunil and Stacey joined the crowds of pupils ambling into school. The idea for making Merrick Hall into a school had come to Barnaby in 1944, when he was in his late seventies.

During the Second World War, Merrick Hall had once more opened its doors to strangers. This time children, dozens of kids evacuated from the cities.

Despite a heart attack earlier, and the fact that he was confined to a wheelchair, Barnaby had still found the time and energy to mingle with the kids. To take an interest.

'Cheeky little blighters call me Granddad,' he had recorded in one of his diaries. 'Such scruffy urchins with their thin faces and grubby knees but they make me smile and, for their sakes, I have to believe that there is hope left in an increasingly hopeless and violent world.'

Later, in a letter to his solicitor, Barnaby had written: 'No doubt you'll think that age has addled my brain but last night, at dusk, as I looked down onto the lawn, I fancied I saw Charles, leaning against the oak tree. He was watching the children play. But the strange thing was, they were not the children of now. They were the children of tomorrow. Thousands of them, stretching far into the future. And the vision reminded me of something I'd been meaning to do...'

158

Brad stood up and stared at the statue, as he recalled Merrick's words. Ghosts. Visions. Had Barnaby really seen the ghost of his son? Had he glimpsed the future? Could he have possessed some psychic power that Colford's disturbed mind had been able to tap into?

Brad shook his head. No, he told himself. Don't even go down that route. Col's communications with Mr Merrick had simply been part of his increasingly desperate fantasy world. And Merrick's statement to his solicitor was merely a figure of speech. A way of explaining why he intended to sign Merrick Hall over as a school. Merrick had some strong views about schools. About the way kids should be treated.

'But you couldn't help Col, could you?' said Brad, scowling at the statue. 'Why did you let it happen, eh? You were supposed to be his friend. Why didn't you stop him?'

The statue stared back with those large, sad eyes. Questioning eyes. Colford's eyes.

'Sure,' said Brad. 'You tried. We all tried. But it wasn't enough, was it, Mr Merrick?'

The statue remained silent. Impassive.

'Talk to me!' Brad shouted. 'Just tell me I'll get through it. Just tell me Col will be all right.'

Merrick didn't speak. But suddenly Brad knew exactly what he'd say if he could. The words he'd said over and over in his letters and diaries.

Brad took a couple of deep breaths, as Stacey had instructed, and for a moment, looking at the statue, he felt totally calm and peaceful, in a way that he hadn't done in months. Were those feelings coming from Merrick or from himself? Was he finally starting to get a grip or cracking up completely?

Getting a grip, he told himself. Definitely. It was the only way. He had to start believing what everyone had been telling him. That Colford wouldn't simply be convicted and stuck in prison for the rest of his life. That his circumstances would be taken into consideration. He'd get help. Treatment. There'd be some sort of future for him. There had to be.

'Hope, right?' Brad said, winking at the statue. 'That's what kept you going, isn't it?'

'Brad!' said Stacey, rushing up and grabbing his arm. 'What are you doing? Please tell me you weren't talking to that statue.'

'I was,' said Brad. 'And, in a funny sort of way, it helped. But I won't make a habit of it, I promise.'

'Good,' said Stacey, as they walked towards the school. 'That's the best bit of news I've heard in a long time.'